Ambush on the Butterfield Trail

When Abednego Merton's young daughter is seized by Comancheros, he resolves to recover his beloved child, no matter what the cost. He also vows privately that he will, in the process, kill every man who had any part, however small, in taking his daughter from him.

Ambush on the Butterfield Trail

Jay Clanton

A Black Horse Western

ROBERT HALE

© Jay Clanton 2019
First published in Great Britain 2019

ISBN 978-0-7198-2997-0

The Crowood Press
The Stable Block
Crowood Lane
Ramsbury
Marlborough
Wiltshire SN8 2HR

www.bhwesterns.com

Robert Hale is an imprint
of The Crowood Press

Typeset by
Derek Doyle & Associates, Shaw Heath
Printed and bound in Great Britain by
4Bind Ltd, Stevenage, SG1 2XT

CHAPTER 1

The covered wagon crawled across the arid and sparsely vegetated plain, following a dusty track that was all but indistinguishable from the surrounding landscape. The two oxen drawing the wagon plodded along as slowly as they were able, only speeding up very slightly when the driver touched them both with his whip, before resuming their earlier and more leisurely pace a few seconds later. The man on the buckboard was a rugged-looking individual of perhaps fifty or sixty years of age. Getting on in years he might have been, but he was still hale and there was a look about his face that suggested that he was not a man to be crossed lightly. This was somebody who knew how to handle himself and was not one to allow others to impose their will upon him.

Seated next to the fellow holding the reins was another person, who was at first harder to read. She had a womanly figure but there was a coltish awkwardness about her, which suggested a child more than it did an adult. Combined with the fact that her skirts did not reach down to her ankles and that she had not yet begun to put up her hair, the impression was given that here was a girl on the cusp of womanhood. Her name was Hannah Merton and she would, if she were spared, be celebrating her sixteenth birthday in something over a month's time.

The visage of the man seated beside the girl might have habitually worn an expression of grim determination, but when he glanced sideways at her, his face was transformed. It was a little like watching the sun rise, as the pleasure and pride that he obviously felt in her drove away the stern lines and watchful look in his eyes. She caught him looking at her and said smilingly, 'What ails you, Pa? Something amiss?'

'Not a thing. I was just thinking how much you're getting to resemble your ma, God rest her, as you get older.'

Hannah looked thoughtful and then said, 'I can't hardly recollect her, you know. Just the look of her eyes, I think, and a smell of lavender. That's the sum of it.'

'You were but knee-high to a grasshopper when she was promoted to glory,' said her father. 'It's not in reason that you should remember much at the age you were.'

'You reckon we'll reach that little town you talked of by nightfall?'

'It'll be a blessing if we do.'

When Abednego Merton and his daughter had set off from Fort Smith in Arkansas, forty days earlier, it had been spring. Now, summer was here in earnest and they were still not halfway to their destination, which was California. It had been Abe Merton, as he was generally known, who had decided that they might make a better fist of things in the west than they had been doing, scraping a living on a small-holding in Arkansas. So it was that he had sold up, fitted out a wagon and struck out from Fort Smith, heading along what was once the Butterfield Overland Mail route running through Texas and into the New Mexico and Arizona territories.

The three years since the end of the War Between the States had been lean ones for many and Abe did not complain. He knew, though, that if his daughter were to have the opportunity to fulfil her promise then she could better achieve that end in a young, energetic place like California than she would grub-bing out her life in the fields of Arkansas. Hannah was sharp as a lancet and it was Abe's hope that it might somehow be possible for her to study, perhaps at college level, in one of the big cities such as San Francisco. It was a dream and he had no idea if it was an attainable one, but he surely meant to try. After all, he thought, what else are our dreams for if not to lead us on and encourage us to try and improve our lot? Despite his deep-seated religious faith, Merton was not one of those who believed that a man should

7

labour on, thankful in the station in which it has pleased the Lord to place him. Although he seldom voiced the view out loud, he was a firm believer in the dictum that the Lord helped those who helped themselves.

Abednego Merton had never been one for depending on other folks, and so had not even considered joining a wagon train when he made the fateful decision at the beginning of 1868 to uproot him and his daughter and head west. He relied on nobody and wanted nobody, other than his child of course, to rely upon him. He had bought and fitted out a wagon, secured a post as an engineer at a manufactory on the west coast and then, with no more ado, harnessed up a pair of oxen and taken to the trail. They were now something in the region of a hundred and fifty miles east of El Paso, which would mark roughly the halfway point in their journey.

Even while he was chatting amiably with his child, Abe's eyes were constantly scanning ahead and to the side, checking for anything out of the ordinary. Thus it was that he caught sight of what he guessed to be a party of riders when they were still some miles off. Judging from the amount of dust being kicked into the air and one or two other points, he calculated that there were at least a half-dozen men and that there were heading straight for the wagon. This made him a mite uneasy, for the riders were not following the track, but were moving towards him from the side, almost as though they had it in mind to intercept the wagon.

'Hannah,' said Merton, 'You get into the wagon, if you please, and hunker down so's you can't be seen.'

'Is something wrong, Pa?'

'I hope not, but better safe than sorry. Go on now, quick as you like.'

Casting a scared look at her father, Hannah scrambled into the back of the wagon and crouched among the household goods that were stowed there.

He had no rifle or shotgun, or else Merton would have had it cocked and in his lap by now. He contented himself with loosening the pistol that he had tucked into his belt and making sure that he could withdraw it swiftly, should need arise. There was no special reason to expect trouble, but this part of Texas nigh to the Rio Grande, which marked the border with Mexico, had somewhat of a lawless reputation, and Abe Merton didn't aim to take any chances. He halted the wagon and then sat waiting for the riders to approach. Maybe then he would see what they were about.

All Abe Merton's hackles rose as the men came close enough for him to see them clearly. There were seven of them and if they weren't on the scout then he was a Dutchman. They had that careless look about them as though they didn't need to worry in the slightest degree what other folk cared to think of them. A couple of them had coppery skins and looked like half-breeds. One of these had hair as long as a woman's, flying free. Two of the other men also had long, shaggy locks and all except the breeds were sporting moustaches. Although they looked pretty wild, it was clear that these boys, none of whom could be much above twenty-five years of age, weren't cowboys, ranch-hands or aught of that kind. They weren't dressed for hard work and all were armed to the teeth. By the time they were within hailing distance, Merton could see that half of them had bandoliers of cartridges slung across their chests and he could see scabbards at the front of their saddles that contained rifles. One or two also had rifles over their backs on slings. His heart sank as they slowed to a sedate trot and spread out as they came closer to the wagon. Pulling his piece would simply result in his death; he was that outnumbered. Then where would that leave Hannah? At the mercy of these scallywags, that's where.

When they were five or ten yards away, the riders halted and one of them greeted Merton in a cheerful enough fashion, saying, 'Afternoon, pilgrim. Where you headed?'

'Over yonder,' replied Merton, gesturing vaguely to the west.

'Cautious sort of fellow, ain't you?' said another of the men, which elicited laughter from the rest. 'What's the matter? Don't you care for our company?'

10

'I don't want for company,' said Merton levelly, 'I'm just hoping to carry on down this track, is all.'

'What you got in that there wagon?' asked one of the riders, 'Something valuable, I'll be bound.'

'Not hardly. Just bits and pieces from my home, as was. I'm removing to California and taking my furniture and suchlike along of me.'

'That a fact?' said one of the other men, mockingly.

'Yes, that's a fact. If you boys've got no objection, I'll be carrying on now.'

'Mind if we look at your gear? Happen we might be able to trade, you know, a bit of buying and selling?'

It struck Merton that one or two of these young men spoke with a slight accent. Not strong, but definitely there all the same. One thing was certain-sure: it was as plain as the nose on his face to Abednego that these fellows had murder and robbery in mind and he saw no way out of the situation. Whether he waited for them to make their move or if he brought matters to the point himself made no odds. Either way, matters were likely to end in the same way. He could see no way of saving Hannah, but now he was out of time because the riders were edging forward, clearly preparing to attack.

If there was to be gunplay, then Abe Merton wanted it to be as far from the wagon as could be. That way, there would be less chance of his daughter being struck by a stray ball. Without giving any sign of his intentions, Merton leapt to his feet and jumped from the buckboard. His action took the men surrounding the wagon by surprise, as did Merton's next move, which was to run straight at the them, passing between two horses before any of them even realized what he was about. As he ran, the desperate man drew the Colt Navy from his belt, cocking it with his thumb as he did so. Having done so, he stopped dead in his tracks, whirled round and fired twice, hitting one of the riders smack between his shoulder blades.

The amazement occasioned by the actions of the man whom they had supposed that they were about to kill wore off with the first shot, and one of the breeds slid the rifle from where it nestled at the front of his saddle. He had done this even before Merton fired and had already worked the lever, feeding a cartridge into the breach when the sound of the shot came. He didn't need to turn his horse; instead he simply swivelled round at the waist and fired straight at the man whose wagon they were determined to loot. He had the satisfaction of seeing the man's shirt whip up as the bullet struck him in the chest, before he dropped lifeless to the ground.

The man who Merton had shot had by this time slumped from his horse. One of the others, who was his particular friend, jumped down to attend to the wounded man, but the case was hopeless. A gout of bright blood had overflowed from his mouth and run all over his chin. From the vivid, crimson hue, it was a fair guess that this blood had come from a wound to the lungs, which meant that there was little hope. This was confirmed when as soon as his friend clasped him in his arms, the fellow who had been shot gave a quiet grunt and promptly died without opening his eyes.

Laying his dead comrade gently to the ground, the man who had just cradled the dying man in his arms stood up and walked over to where Abednego Merton lay motionless and then swung his boot at the prone man's head. Merton's shirt was bloody all over the front and there was every sign that he was dead, but the angry man kicked him again and again. Then somebody shouted to him, 'Rafe, come over here now. This'n will maybe soften your sorrow!'

The others had now dismounted and were clustered around the back of the wagon. They were peering in with looks of delight upon their faces, for there, cowering within, was a frightened young girl. Crude exclamations of pleasure and delight were being made, before the man who was nominally in charge of their party said, 'Come, get her down now. See if there's anything else worth having here. It looks to me like a heap o' shit.'

After the girl was dragged screaming from the wagon, her cries redoubling in intensity when she saw her father laying on his back and covered in blood, the men clambered up and began throwing out the Mertons' belongings. Items such as bedding and a few meagre pieces of furniture were discarded contemptuously. Their only interest lay in cash money or valuables such as jewellery. Finding nothing of the sort, they abandoned the search and turned to look at the girl, who was being gripped firmly by the arm, lest she attempt to flee.

'None o' that,' said the man who was directing the scouting party, 'Not a one of you need think it for a moment.'

'We can touch her though,' observed one of the others, 'That won't spoil the goods.'

'Not while I have breath in my body, you won't,' said the leader. 'I seed with my own eyes where this "touching" ends and the last time it cost us all dear. Leave her be, I say.'

For a moment when she heard these words, Hannah Merton thought that she had found a pro-tector, one among these inhuman wretches to whom she might appeal to behave with decency, but she was all too soon disabused of this notion. The man who had forbidden any of the others to touch her went over to his horse and, after rummaging in his saddle-bag, returned with a length of rope. While two others held the girl securely, he lashed her wrists together and then ran the rope down to her ankles and tied them also. This process was accomplished with as no more acknowledgement of the girl than if she had been a mustang or hog. After checking the knots, the

14

leader picked up the girl, who was too frightened to resist, and slung her over the front of his saddle. He said, 'Let's go, boys!'

The band of men mounted and then made off, back in the direction from which they had come. Hannah Merton lay face down, her arms dangling on one side of the saddle and her legs on the other. What was to become of her she had not the faintest idea. Her thoughts turned to her father, laying in the dirt and covered in blood, and she began to weep hopelessly and without restrain, like a child.

It was late afternoon, two hours or so after the ambush. The contents of the wagon lay strewn about. Some articles, such as the beautiful pendulum clock, which had been a wedding gift to the Mertons on the occasion of their marriage seventeen years earlier, lay smashed in the roadway. In their anger at finding nothing worth stealing, the bandits had kicked and thrown around the precious belongings, wantonly destroying for the pure sake of it. A cloud of flies swirled in a lazy cloud over the figure laying some way off from the looted wagon. They were feasting on the blood that had oozed from the man's face and saturated his shirt. In another hour or so, they would be laying their eggs there.

To any observer of the scene, what happened at this point would have looked like some latter-day Lazarus, arising from the tomb. The man groaned and then raised his arm to shoo the flies from his face. Then, after a pause of a minute or so, he sat up. It came as a great surprise to Abednego Merton to find that he was still in the land of the living, and for a while he couldn't make the thing at all. He had a distinct recollection of being shot in the heart and also of being kicked in the face. It was that blow which had rendered him unconscious, but he had already decided that he was about to die from the wound to his chest. It was all most perplexing.

Slowly, and with great pain, Merton moved his hands to his chest and felt around a bit. Every breath he drew was agonising, but there could be not the least doubt that he was drawing breath and was therefore not dead. His ribs were excessively tender on the left side, right above his heart, and Merton feared to look. Nevertheless, he undid his shirt slowly and looked down at his chest. There was a deal of blood, but not as much as he would have expected, had his heart been smashed to atoms by a minie ball, which was what he had supposed to have happened. Spitting on his fingers, Merton smeared away some of the congealed blood and the mystery was solved. The ball had not struck him not full in the chest, which would inevitably have resulted in his death, but had rather taken him at a shallow angle. It had certainly cracked a couple of ribs and gouged a deep furrow in the muscles and flesh of his chest, which accounted for the great amount of blood, but he was otherwise whole.

Having established that he was alive, Abednego Merton lurched to his feet and stumbled across to the wagon, seeking any sign of his daughter. There was none: those who had accosted him had evidently taken the child. As usual when he was troubled, Merton turned to God for guidance. Moreover, he thought it only fitting to give thanks to the Lord for his deliverance. Carefully and with several cries of anguish at the pain in his injured ribs, he managed to kneel there on the dusty track and addressed the deity in the following words: 'Lord, I thank you for sparing my life, which was unlooked for. I should o' shot my child, 'fore I let her be took off by those villains for who knows what purpose. I'm greatly to blame for not having thought on it. I beseech your help now, Lord, in tracking down those as did this dreadful thing and rescuing my little girl from their clutches. And I swear now, I will kill every one of those who had any hand in this matter. Amen.'

The wounded man remained on his knees for a spell, to give the Lord time to respond, if He was so minded, but there was only silence. The question now was what course of action should he now follow? It would be madness to follow riders on foot; that much was certain. No, Merton knew that his first task was to acquire a horse. He looked at the two oxen and shook his head. Even at their fastest, oxen are among the slowest of God's creatures and riding one of them would be no better than going by shank's pony. The town to which they had been heading was perhaps five miles away and even as he was, Merton guessed that he could do that in better than a couple of hours.

Before leaving the site of the disaster that had befallen him and his girl, Merton turned loose the oxen and then, using some of the linen that had been scattered on the ground, he bound up his ribs as tight as he could bear. It eased the pain when he drew breath a little, although it was still going to be a hard journey. Then he started walking west.

It was heavy going, for apart from his ribs there had been a nasty blow to his head with a boot, which had left Merton with a terrible headache and the fear that the kick had effected some mischief to his skull. There was little to be done about it though. Worse than the physical pain was the mental anguish of knowing that he had failed his daughter in the worst possible way. If only he had thought to end her life before she had been captured, rather than point-lessly shooting one of the band. He would have to live with this guilt, he supposed.

In spite of the pain he was in, it took Abednego Merton just an hour and a half to reach the hamlet or town for which he and his daughter had been headed. To his surprise, Merton saw that there was an army encampment by the town and this gave him reason to hope that he might get some assistance in recovering his daughter. Before entering the town, he approached the sentry standing guard at the line of tents and asked if he could be conducted to their commanding officer. The man on guard duty called to a passing trooper and asked if he would show this civilian gentleman to the major's tent.

Major Travers listened gravely to Abe Merton's account of what had befallen him. At the end of it he said, 'It's a damned shame and that's a fact. But I don't quite see why you've come to tell me about it. This is a civil matter. You want a sheriff or marshal.'

'You have men here who could ride after those men, don't you?'

'To put the case bluntly, I've other fish to fry. I'm sorry, it can't be done.'

'She's an innocent child!' said Merton wonderingly. 'You won't raise a hand to help her?'

The major did not like being blustered or buffaloed in this way by a civilian, but all the same he could not help but feel sympathetic. He said slowly, 'Truth is, we're on the track of people like those who took your daughter. They're most likely Comancheros, working with the Kiowa hereabouts. There's nests of 'em all over this part of Texas.'

As Merton began to interrupt, suggesting that in that case their aims coincided, Major Travers held up his hand and said, 'Wait now. Listen to what I say. I can't go haring after one group or another of those fellows. They're holed up in some canyons with their

19

Indian friends. I'd need a damn sight more men than I have here and a couple of field guns into the bargain were I to launch a frontal assault on them. I'm skirmishing with them though and waiting for Washington to order reinforcements. Till then, there's nothing I can do.'

'Why do you think they took my girl?' asked Merton in a dull and flat voice, 'Apart that is from the usual reason men like them snatch women and girls.'

'Sometimes, they ransom their captives,' said the major, 'See if the relatives can raise a tidy sum, you know.'

'I ain't got but a few dollars to my name. What do they ask in such cases?'

The major shrugged. 'It depends. A few hundred dollars at the very least.'

'And if they don't get it?'

Major Travers fidgeted and seemed reluctant to answer the question. Merton stared silently at him, until the major finally said awkwardly, 'There's a, ahem, you might call it a market for girls, especially young ones. Across the Rio Grande, you know.'

'Market? What are you talking of?'

'To set the case out plainly, young white girls, such as have never laid with a man, well, they fetch a fair price in some . . . establishments down in Mexico. They smuggle them across the river, near El Paso. Here, hold up, man!'

20

This last remark was caused by Abednego Merton turning dead white and staggering, as though he were about to fall. The major said, 'Rest here a while. From the look of you, you're in no fit state to do anything right now.'

Casting the soldier a look of blazing contempt, Merton straightened up and said, 'I'm a-going for to fetch my daughter back. You say you won't help. All I can say is that young men today are a sight different from what they once were. Won't even go to the aid of a helpless child.' Having delivered himself of these parting words, he turned on his heel and left the tent.

CHAPTER 2

Abednego Merton was a native of Arkansas and had been raised there, in grinding poverty, with his family. Somehow, they contrived to make enough food on a forty-acre holding in the western part of the territory, near Fort Smith. As soon as he was old enough, young Abe escaped by joining the army. This was in 1827, when he was just sixteen years of age. Of course, he lied about his age; not that it really mattered to the recruiting sergeant. He was a stout farm boy who could handle a musket and that was all that was needful at that time to be a soldier in the army.

It was an interesting period to be in the army, and after joining in June, Merton found himself being sent north to Wisconsin almost immediately to fight in the Winnebago war against the Ho-Chunk Indians. He was present when their leader Red Bird was captured, and from then on young Merton was pretty generally recognized as a good man to have by your side when the going got hot.

For over twenty years, Abe Merton fought his way across various parts of the United States, fighting Indians and Mexicans, sometimes white men and at other times red. When he was thirty-eight years old and had worked his way up to sergeant, he received word that his father had died and that his mother was ailing. So Abe Merton left the army and went back to his childhood home in Arkansas. His mother was indeed ailing, for she died within a month of his return, leaving Merton as sole possessor of the little farm. Six months later, he and a young girl of just eighteen, the daughter of a neighbour, fell in love and married. Nobody looked for so great a disparity of age to lead to mutual harmony and marital happiness, but they were quite wrong. Abe and his new bride Elizabeth were blissfully content, even though life was hard and money scarce.

Because it took something over eighteen months for Elizabeth to fall pregnant, the couple feared that there might be some difficulty, for if the young girl had not yet conceived it was not from want of trying on their part. Because she was as devout and God-fearing as Abednego himself, when she finally did bear a child more than two years after they were wed, she wished to christen the child Hannah, after the prophet Samuel's mother in the Bible, whose womb the Lord had opened up.

For the next three years, the family thrived. Poor in material goods they might have been, but overflowing in riches if you counted love and affection as signifying more in the great scheme of things than diamonds and gold. There was no brother or sister for little Hannah, which was from time to time a source of grief, but that apart they were as happy as the day is long. Until, that is, Elizabeth was struck down with the bloody flux in the fall of 1856. She died within the week.

Raising a child by himself while running a farm was no easy task but, with the assistance of Elizabeth's family and a little help from other neighbours, Merton managed it well enough. The War Between the States was a rough time, but still he and his daughter got by. After three years of martial law and reconstruction though, Abednego Merton had had enough and with the offer of a job in California, and the hope of better prospects for his daughter's education, he lit out west along the Butterfield Overland Trail until misfortune overtook him when he was not halfway through his journey.

The town of Endeavour was too small to boast a sheriff. There was a local vigilance committee, which from time to time took the law into their own hands and delivered beatings and the occasional hanging to malefactors who troubled the area, but their concerns were strictly parochial. They cared only about offences against their own citizens that occurred

24

within a mile or two of town. Merton discovered this when he went hunting for some official body to aid him in the recovery of his child. The storekeepers to whom he spoke were sympathetic, but did not at all think it likely that anybody in the town would be prepared to risk his neck for the sake of a stranger. They did not state this out loud, but that was the gist of what Merton gleaned as he made his way along the town's main street. It was just as he had suspected: he would have to undertake the job by his own self.

There were few stores in Endeavour, the largest of which was the hardware store that, in addition to the usual buckets, pails, brooms, household tools and ironmongery, sold firearms. Some were new, but others were left over from the late war; many former soldiers found that they would rather have the money for a square meal than hang on to a carbine for the sake of sentiment. It was fortunate, reflected Merton, that he had been left not only with his life, but also his pistol. He figured though that he would also need a rifle before this enterprise had come to an end and since those who had stolen away his daughter had not seen fit to search what they supposed to be his corpse, he also had over $100 in gold coins sewed into his britches.

'How may I help you this day, sir?' asked the storekeeper, although looking a little askance at the man who walked into the premises just before he was planning on closing for the day. Had he but known

it, Abe Merton presented a grim aspect, with his shirt
torn and besmeared with gore and his face bruised
and cut about it.

'I'm seeking a musket. A rifle, you know. One as is
good for distance shooting.'

'Well, sir, we've a fine selection for you to make
your choice from. Rifles and carbines are, as you
may say, a drag on the market these days and you can
have your pick of quite a few. Or were you looking
for something new? We got Winchester Yellowboys if
so.'

'I don't take kindly to Winchesters. What have you
for distance work?'

'Military, you mean?'

'I ain't so fussed. Show me what you have.'

The storekeeper went to the room at back of the
counter and emerged with two rifles. One was an
unremarkable carbine, but the other was of very
unusual design indeed. Merton's eyes lit up when he
caught sight of this and he exclaimed, 'A Whitworth,
by Godfrey! The very thing.'

'You know this weapon? I confess, somebody sold
it me three years ago and it's been languishing in the
back there since. I never saw the like of it except this
once.'

'I don't wonder at it. It's British,' said Merton, as
he took the gun in his hands and examined it carefully, sighting down the barrel and checked the
hammer. 'It sights to twelve-hundred yards, but you

26

can be accurate above that if you know how to handle it.'

'You don't say so.'

'I do. It's what I want. What are you asking?'

'Well now, I guess I rather shot myself in the foot,' said the clerk ruefully, 'letting on that it's been around for so long without selling. You'll be 'specting a bargain price, I'll warrant.'

Merton looked up impatiently and said, 'I'm kind o' in a hurry, so just tell me what you want.'

'Say twenty dollars and I'll throw in a box of caps. It's a muzzle-loader, you know.'

'You sell powder too?'

'Surely. You'll want balls for it too, I dare say.'

When he had concluded his business in the hardware store, Merton went down the street to the livery stable at the end and there purchased a tough little mare, along with tack for the same. A loaf of bread, some dried meat and cheese, and he was ready to leave.

Strange to relate, the conversation that he had had with the major in charge of the troops camped outside town had served to reassure Merton, once he realized what the officer had been driving at. Although he had never visited a cathouse in his life, he had heard before that a premium was set upon virgins. Apart from the fact that some brutal reprobates gained pleasure from the experience of what they were pleased to call 'breaking a girl in', there

27

was the other matter. Laying with a girl who had not yet known a man was said to be, according to legend that is, a sovereign remedy for the pox and other diseases to which promiscuous and degraded men were prone.

Horrible though it was to consider such things in relation to his beloved child, it meant that she was not in present danger of being ravished by any of the bandits who had taken her. Her value would diminish sharply if, on delivery to the brothel, she was found not to be intact. This meant that it was in the long-term interest of those varmints to make sure that she was not the subject of carnal lust while she was in their hands.

As he rode out of town, Merton tried to recall what he had heard about the present state of affairs in Texas. He had known before they set out that there was some species of trouble with the Kiowa and Comanche, but he'd had the notion that this was more serious to the north of the state, rather than along the parts near the Mexican border where he would be going. He'd had dealings with Comancheros in the past, during his army days, but again had believed their depredations to be more common in the north. These were men outside the usual rules of society, vicious brutes even by the standards of the average outlaw. Many men who lived by robbery adhered to a code of their own, similar in some ways to the chivalry of the old-time knights, but there was nothing of this kind with the Comancheros. The rattlesnake code held that you always had to give warning before you struck, just like the snake, and that it was cowardly and unmanly to attack without warning. It was also frowned upon to trouble women or children. The Comancheros did not worry about such niceties.

In fact, Abe Merton had been a little troubled in his mind as to whether he had behaved honourably himself by shooting that man in the back. Although he had acted on the spur of the moment and in what he believed to be the best way of preserving his daughter's life, it went very much against the grain for Merton to shoot a man in the back. As he rode northeast towards where he supposed the Comancheros to have their lair, he mulled this over in his mind.

Those boys had really been delivering a challenge when they stopped him, and they must surely have known that when he jumped down from the buck-board like that he was signalling clearly that he was about to attack. His actions could not be compared with those of a man who hides in wait and then guns down a man from behind when he is passing. No, on reflection, he found that his conscience was clear on the matter, and as for the fellow he had killed. . . . Well, his blood was upon his own head.

It was while musing in this fashion that Abe Merton became aware of a rider ahead of him. Since he was not on any track but riding across the barren, dusty plain, this was a noteworthy circumstance. What was even more noteworthy was that this other rider had stopped and was seemingly waiting for Merton to catch up with him. If it was an ambush, then it was a very clumsily laid and ineffectual one. On the other hand, what innocent reason could a man have for setting there on his horse, waiting for a stranger to catch up with him? But Merton thought to himself that it could be a hundred and one things: from a fellow wanting company, on account of they were both heading in the same direction, to something as simple as a man who'd run out of Lucifers and was dying for a smoke! There was no cause to think that whoever was waiting up ahead meant him ill. Nevertheless, Merton reached out his pistol and drew back the hammer to half cock. If there were to be any lively action, then the slightest fraction of a second could make the difference twixt life and death. He tucked it back as loose as could be in his belt.

As he drew closer, Merton saw that the man on the horse was really little more than a boy. He could scarcely be above seventeen or eighteen years of age. Of course, that didn't greatly signify. He himself had killed his first man at the age of sixteen; youth alone was no guarantee of pacific intentions. When he was a dozen yards from the boy, Merton halted and hailed him in a friendly enough fashion, saying,

'Well, you're a young enough fellow to be heading along this trackless waste!'

These cheery words had an unfortunate effect upon the youth, for he immediately snatched up the pistol hanging from his waist and said in a low, harsh voice, 'You making game of me? You're a funny one and I don't think!'

'Whoa there, son . . .' began Merton, at this unlooked for development, 'Steady with that gun now.'

'I ain't your son, nor nothing like, I hope. I reckon you're one of 'em.'

'One of what? I don't have the pleasure of understanding you.'

'Don't fool with me now. Where you going?'

'Just away over yonder.'

The youngster had a hard and determined way about him and Abe Merton wondered despairingly if he was destined to fail in his quest before it had properly begun, at the hands of some young desperado who was hardly old enough to shave.

'Get down from your horse. Real slow, like,' the boy said.

'All right, don't you get twitchy now. See, I'm a doing as you bid.' Matching the action to the words, Abe Merton dismounted, still unsure of the play. Was this young man a Comanchero or what? He somehow didn't have that air about him, but there, you couldn't really tell what was in a man's heart

31

from the look of him or after a few seconds of discourse. Still, it was something that he hadn't shot Merton out of hand. For that at least he was thankful to providence!

As Merton had got down from his horse, the young man had urged on his own mount at a walk, all the while never allowing his aim to falter or waver. The horse halted about six feet from Merton and the fellow said, 'Take out that pistol of your'n from your belt real slow and drop it to the ground.' When Merton had done so, he continued. 'Now that rifle slung over your shoulder, but slowly now; I got you covered good.'

'It's an unwieldy article and I'd as soon not dash it to the ground,' said Merton. 'Truth to tell, I only lately acquired it. Let me just lay it down gentle.' Without waiting to hear if that course of action was agreeable, he slowly removed the musket and bent down to set it gently to the ground. As he did so, he contrived to pick up a handful of dust and stones. Then moving with lightning speed, he stood up and hurled the dirt into the boy's face, while jinking to one side. The pistol went off and the ball flew more closely to Merton's head than was pleasant, but then he had leapt forward and grasped the wrist holding the gun. This, he proceeded to twist it back, until it was close to cracking. Then he used his other hand to remove the weapon from the boy's grasp and cast it to one side. Still gripping the wrist, he wrestled the youngster down from his horse and threw him to the ground. While he was laying there winded, Merton snatched up his own pistol and, backing away from the prone figure so that he was himself out of reach of any sudden attack, said, 'Let's you and me converse a little, son, 'fore I decide whether or not I should shoot you down like dog.'

'I knew you was one of 'em all along!' said the young man laying on the ground, his voice tinged with melancholy satisfaction at his own perspicacity, 'I just knowed it for sure.'

'One of who?' enquired Merton in exasperation, 'I ain't got the least idea of what you're talking about.'

'Why, one of them damned villains as snatched away my sister. You got that look about you, like you'd stick at naught.'

The true state of affairs now dawned on Abe Merton, and if his own case were not so desperate then he might have laughed out loud. He said, 'You think I'm a Comanchero? Just take a close look at me, boy. I'm nearer to sixty than I am fifty. Why, I'm old enough for to be your grandpappy! Comanchero, indeed! Now make haste and tell me what you're about, for I'm in a rare hurry.'

The youngster looked at the older man with uncertainty and said slowly, 'We live some ten miles from here, other side of Endeavour. You know it?'

'The town? Just come from there. Get on, the day's wearing away and it'll be dark soon.'

'We farm a little land. My pa's dead, so it's just me and Ma and my sister. The trouble with the Kiowa and such hasn't reached us here, so it's been safe enough. Three days gone, I went to town with my ma to buy some wares. My sister was doing work about the house. When we got back, she was gone. Neighbour of ours, he told us that some men had been seen thereabouts and little by little, we found out what's what. Heard of those Comancheros before, but never knew they were so close.'

'Happen some bands of them are moving south,' said Merton. 'Maybe the fighting up north is getting too hot for 'em. Go on.'

'Well, then I asked a few folk and learned what they get up to sometimes, taking girls and suchlike. My ma, she's broken up with grief and can't do a thing, so I come to take back my sister.'

'How old is she? Meaning your sister.'

'She's just fourteen.'

Abednego Merton's face twisted in disgust. He'd never heard the like, taking a little girl like that. Still and all, he had his own fish to fry. He said, 'Listen to me now, son. You wouldn't stand a chance going up against such men by your own self. My advice to you is to ride on back to your ma and comfort her. I guess she needs you now more than ever she did before.'

'Go back to my ma? It isn't to be thought of. No, I'm riding on. I reckon those skunks have their lair in those canyons, up in the hills over north.'

34

It was a delicate situation. Sympathetic as he was for the boy's trouble, Abe Merton had no intention of allowing this green youth to go stirring up the Lord knew what trouble and alerting the bandits that there were men after them. It would wreck his own plans. He said, 'What's your name?'

'Edward, but most everybody calls me Ed.'

'Then listen to me, Ed. It would be sheer murder for you to ride against those boys. All that would happen is that your mother would lose her son as well as a daughter. That ain't what you want at all, to increase her suffering and grief. Ride back home now and comfort her. The army are going to be taking some species of action against those Comancheros right soon. Maybe it'll work out for the best and your sister will be freed.'

His words sounded awful thin to Merton and also to the boy, who said sharply, 'What's your part in all this? Where are you headed?'

'That don't signify. Never mind about what I'm doing, nor where I'm bound, neither. Just get yourself home now. Come, I've business to attend to.'

'Why,' said Ed, with a sudden realization, 'You're after them yourself, ain't you? Have they took somebody dear to you?'

'Never mind about that. Just ride back towards town.'

'The hell I will! You can't stop me and I tell you straight, I aim to ride on north.'

It struck Merton that the boy must be very young and inexperienced in the ways of the world to make the claim that he, Abe Merton, couldn't stop him proceeding north. The easiest way, of course, would be to shoot either the horse or its rider and there would be an end to the business, but he knew that he could not bring himself to take such a dreadful action. Out loud, he said, 'This is a damned nuisance!'

'Take me with you,' said the boy, 'Two'd have more chance than one and we could work together to the same end.'

'I don't need a partner, and if I did, I wouldn't choose a youngster like you. How old are you anyways?'

'Coming up to sixteen in a month.'

'You're only fifteen years of age? Lord a-mercy, I can't lead a child into danger. Just go home, son.'

'You'll have to kill me if you want to stop me, else I'm riding on.'

For a moment or two, Merton gave serious thought to just shooting the boy's horse and then riding off and leaving him alone out in the wilderness, but in his heart of hearts, he knew that he could not take such a dishonourable action. Nor could he allow this young fellow to ride off alone and perhaps alarm the men that Merton was hoping to catch unawares. At last, he said, 'Get on your horse, we'll go on together to the foot of those hills and then see what's what.'

The kid was like a puppy who'd been offered a treat, for he said with a grin on his face, 'You won't regret it, sir. I guess we'll make a fine team.'

'Team?' growled Merton irritably. 'Let me tell you now, we're not going for to play baseball. Just mount up.'

As they rode forward towards the hills, which lay perhaps three or for miles north of them, Abe Merton watched anxiously for signs of any lookout that might be posted on some high point of ground. He could see nothing, but that didn't mean much, for a man sitting still on the hillside would be nigh on invisible at this distance. At a guess though, if there were a fair number of the bandits, then they would not be at all close to the plain. Most likely they would have a camp in some valley or hollow. He seemed to recollect that the major to whom he had spoken made mention of canyons. He said to the boy at his side, 'You ever been in yon hills?'

'Yes, but not for a year or two. There was fighting up there during the war. Me and some friends we rode out there after the war ended and found a heap of old stuff, bayonets and what have you, that had been left by the army.'

'Just a plain "Yes" would have done. If you and me are to get on, you haven't to let your mouth run on so. Tell me briefly, what's the land's like up there?'

'It's smooth, white rock. Limestone, somebody said. It's like a maze up there, with narrow channels

37

and little canyons.'

'That's promising.'

They rode on in silence, the boy holding his tongue for fear of being snubbed again. When they were at the base where the hills began and the ground sloped up, Merton said, 'I don't see that I can be rid of you, short of murder. If we're to stay together, then let's get one thing clear as day right now. You do just exactly what I say, with no questions or argument. You apprehend my meaning?'

The young man looked a little nervous now that they might be on the very doorstep of the Comancheros and, despite his gruff and forbidding manner, was glad of the older man's company. He said, 'Yes, sir, I understand.'

'There's no "sir" in the case. My name's Abe, so you can call me by it. We're going to find somewhere to hole up for the night. Not here though.'

'Why not, sir? I mean Abe.'

'I can do without questions too. This here, where we are, is right between the track I was following to El Paso and wherever those scoundrels have their base. I reckon they pass this way tolerable often.'

By riding west for a while and following the contour of the hills, the two of them came eventually to a cliff, which had at its base a jumble of boulders and scree. There was space enough for the two of them to lay down there, and the horses would also be out of view of the plain. It wasn't a perfect arrangement, for neither Merton nor his young partner had any notion where in the hills the Comancheros might be; for all they knew to the contrary, this could be the very spot where they came to and from their base. But it was twilight and Merton felt that he needed a good night's sleep before taking action the next day. Oddly enough, young Ed's tale had been encouraging, for it suggested that those boys were trying to get together a fair bunch of girls before taking them all down to the Rio Grande at one go and somehow getting them across into Mexico. This would make a conspicuous caravan and there would surely be a chance to stop them in their tracks.

Once the horses were hobbled and the two of them were seated behind the screen of boulders, Merton found to his surprise that he was pretty hungry. He said, 'You got food with you, son?'

'Yes. You think we should light a fire?'

'Are you plumb out of your mind?'

'Yeah, maybe it's not such a good scheme,' said Ed, not at all abashed. 'Then I guess we'll have to be content with cold vittles.'

'That you will.'

They shared some of the bread and cheese that Merton had, along with some fruit and a meat pie, which Ed provided. As they ate, Ed said, 'That's a strange rifle you got. What's that tube atop of the barrel?'

'Telescope. Helps to see better for distance work.'

'You said you'd only just got it though. Have you had one before?'

'I have.'

It would have been plain to a grown-up person that Abednego Merton had no wish to answer a heap of questions, but the young man did not seem to notice. He continued, 'You in the war? My pa was killed fighting.'

'I'm sorry to hear it.'

'Well, were you? In the war?'

It struck Merton that it was time to put an end to all these foolish questions, but so eager and good natured was young Ed that he couldn't bring himself to be harsh with him. On the other hand, he had no desire to reminisce about the late war. He contented himself with saying, 'I played my part in the war, such as it was. It ain't specially a topic I'm anxious to visit, so if it's all the same with you, we'll avoid it.'

'Oh, surely. Truth is, my pa was fighting for the Confederacy. I was only wondering what side you'd o' been on.'

'Lord a-mercy, son, will you let it alone now? If you will have it, then I was on the same side. But don't go asking me what unit I was in or anything of that sort. I don't know about you, but it's almost dark now and I aim for to get some sleep. I earnestly recommend that you take a similar course of action.'

'Yeah, I guess I am a bit tired. Goodnight, sir.'

'Goodnight, son.'

40

CHAPTER 3

At first light, Abe Merton awoke and for a brief moment did not recollect the shocking events of the previous day. Then he remembered that his child was in the worst danger imaginable and his heart felt like a stone. He was not a man though to dwell on his troubles to no purpose, and so he arose and wandered off around the side of the little cliff in order to make water in privacy. Old habit caused him to reach out for his pistol and tuck it in his belt before moving off. While he leaned against the rock-face, waiting for this sluggish, old man's bladder to go into action, Merton caught a glimpse of movement to his right. He did not signal his presence by turning his head or moving his body, but simply swivelled his eyes and saw that a man was creeping up to where Merton had left his young companion slumbering.

A horse stood on the plain below and Merton comprehended precisely what had chanced at once.

A rider had been heading into the hills and caught sight of Merton and the boy's horses. This fellow had then dismounted and come to investigate. From the corner of his eye, Merton observed the man as he made his way cautiously up the slope to where Ed lay. As soon as the stranger moved out of sight, so that the heap of boulders obscured him from view, Merton moved swiftly. He trod, cat-like and delicately, across the loose scree and then very slowly climbed up one of the boulders. Before reaching the top, he took the gun from his belt and cocked it very slowly, so that there was no harsh, metallic click to indicate to the man below that there was anybody in the vicinity, other than the sleeping youth.

Just as he had expected, the man had drawn a pistol of his own and was now moving towards Ed, who was snoring gently. Merton noticed that the young man who had lately arrived had not one but two pistols hanging from a fancy tooled-leather rig. Without the shadow of a doubt, this meant that he was a gunman or bandit of some kind. Mentally, Abe Merton gave a snort of derision. Two pistols were a show-off stunt and waste of weight. One gun was plenty, if you knew how to handle it.

Young Ed's slumber was rudely disturbed by being prodded hard in the ribs by a boot. He opened his eyes to find that he was covered by a villainous-looking fellow who couldn't have been above three or four years older than Ed himself. This young man

42

said, 'Where's your partner?'

'Partner, what partner?'

'Don't fool with me. There's two horses, two saddles here. Where is he?'

'Right here, son, and got the drop on you,' said Merton. 'Best you set down that pistol.'

Without looking round, the man said, 'What say I shoot your partner? I can do that, even if you fire on me.'

'Go right ahead,' replied Merton and there was an unmistakable note of sincerity in his tone. 'He's nothing to me. Shoot him if you will, but I promise if you don't put that weapon down, you're a dead man.'

The intruder had a strong survival instinct and knew that he was likely to be killed if he didn't do as he had been bid. He guessed that before he even turned to try and find his target, the other man would shoot him down. There was a deadly edge to the voice of the unseen man that suggested that he wasn't prone to issuing baseless threats. Very slowly, he bent down and placed his pistol on the ground.

'Ed, you take up your own gun and watch this fellow. Any sign of movement, if he so much as farts, you kill him.'

Nothing loth to turn the tables on the man who had caught him unawares, the youngster did as Merton had said and soon had the other man covered. Merton called down, 'Now. You, mister

43

fancy gunman, you set on the ground away from your pistol, and with your back to my friend there. Put both your hands on your head.' Sullenly, the intruder did as he was told.

After scrambling down from the rocks, Merton clambered down and joined Ed. His ribs hurt damnably and he hoped that he had not made the injuries that he had suffered the previous day any worse. The pain did nothing to sweeten his temper towards his prisoner. Keeping his gun pointing at the man, he said to Ed, 'Scoot over to my saddle-bag there. You'll find a few lengths of rawhide. Fetch me one, if you will.' When Merton had the thin strip of leather, he went over to his prisoner and lashed his wrists together scientifically. He drew the bonds so tight that the man winced and said, 'You needn't act so. You got the upper hand. . . .' to which Merton responded with a mirthless chuckle.

After removing the second pistol from its holster and checking the man over to ensure that he had no knives or Derringers concealed about his person, Abe Merton stood in front of the man and said, 'In the army, I was reckoned to be a good man at extracting information from prisoners. Only thing was, some of them didn't live long after I was through with them.' He said this not in a boastful or threatening way, but as casually as though he were talking of having once been a shoemaker or clerk.

'Now,' continued Merton, 'I need to know how

many men are hid over in those hills, what prisoners they have and what their intentions are. I want to know when they're setting off for the border, you understand me?'

The seated man spat at Merton's feet and asked rhetorically, 'You think I'd betray my comrades?'

What struck Ed afterwards was that Abe Merton did not ask another question at all, nor debate with the fellow in any way whatsoever. He simply proceeded to beat him. Now Ed had seen fights and even taken part in a few. This was something else, though. Using only his fists and feet, the older man worked over the prisoner methodically. He began by bending down and punching his victim in the mouth with all the not inconsiderable strength at his disposal. Then, when the man was knocked backwards, Merton went up to him and stamped hard on his shin, causing the man to yelp like a scalded cat. Then Merton hauled him upright again and spent a minute landing heavy blows on the face and ribs, interspersed with kicks on vulnerable parts of the body such as the hands. It was sickening to watch and Ed turned away.

It took just two minutes of this treatment before the prisoner repented of his pledge to say nothing and began babbling like a child. The turning point came when an especially vicious kick of Merton's, aimed at the fellow's forearm, resulted in a sharp crack, like a dry stick being snapped in two. Ed knew instinctively that this meant that his arm had just been broken.

'There's a dozen or more of us up there. We got girls, eleven, twelve, I don't rightly know. God's sake, free me. My arm's broke.'

'When you headed for the border?' asked Abe Merton implacably, ' 'Less you want me to break your other arm.'

'Tomorrow, maybe the next day.'

'Not today?'

'No, we're waiting for another group to join us; they've been huntin' for more girls.'

'How many in this other party?'

'Six, seven.'

Merton thought this over for a spell and then said, 'So the full strength of your little company is something less than twenty, once these others have arrived, is that right?'

'Yes. Now, for God's sake, set me free. Take my weapons. I need to get help for my arm.'

'You transporting the girls in carts?'

'Yes. Let me free, please. I beg of you.'

Abednego Merton stood there, his face impassive, as though he had not heard this desperate appeal. Then he said to his young partner, 'Gather up our things and tack up the horses, if you would. I got something needs doing.'

'What about me?' wailed the man lying in the dirt. 'You going to have mercy on me?'

Without answering, Merton walked down the slope until he came to the man's horse, which was a beautiful bay mare. He led her up to the boulders where her owner was laying and looking pretty sorry for himself. At the sight of his mount his eyes lit up, as he supposed that Merton was about to free him and allow him to leave with his life.

Once Ed had their horses ready to go and their gear stashed in saddle-bags, Merton went over to his own mount and removed a razor-sharp blade from the saddle-bag, something in the style of a Bowie knife. He drew this from its sheath and walked over to the mare and patted it softly on the neck. Then he turned his head to the boy with whom he had recently picked up and said, 'If you're in any way squeamish, you best look away now.'

'You can't mean to harm that creature!' cried Ed, with genuine distress in his face. 'Why, it's done you no ill. Can't you just turn it loose?'

'And have this wretch's riderless horse advertise his presence here? No, I don't think so.'

'But you can't . . .' said the boy and then recoiled in horror as Merton drew the knife across the horse's throat, cutting deep and severing both the major artery which lay there and also the beast's windpipe. Blood jetted out and the animal gave a terrified whinny and reared up a little, before its rear legs gave way and it sank to the ground. All the while, Merton stayed at the creature's side, a sad look upon his face.

47

When the mare had breathed its last, Merton turned to his helpless prisoner, the knife in his hand dripping gore. From the look on his face, it was clear that the fellow whose arm he had broken believed that he was about to have his throat cut with no more ceremony than had been accorded to his mount. Seeing the look, Merton smiled grimly and said, 'I ain't going for to cut your throat, you can make yourself easy on that score.'

'What you going to do then?'

'Nothing at all, said Merton mildly. 'Well, beyond gagging you so's you can't cry out for aid, that is.'

'You ain't going to leave me here to die?'

'I reckon so. Unless you want me to put a ball through your head before leaving. . . . Save you the suffering of dying by inches of thirst.'

There was something so extraordinarily cold and impassive about the way that Merton spoke that the man upon whom he had virtually pronounced a death sentence stared at him in wonder and asked, 'What kind of man are you?'

The reply was calm and unemotional. 'I'm the kind of man whose precious child was snatched from him by a band of ruffians and who means to be revenged upon every mother's son of them. You're getting off light on account of your age. I reckon in this heat, you'll pass out in a few hours and be dead with a day or two. Your friends might not be so fortunate.'

During this conversation, Ed stood stock still, believing that his companion was setting out to frighten the other man witless and that at the last he would cut his bonds and leave him to walk to Endeavour with his broken arm. He did not for moment think that any man could be so inhuman as to condemn another to a lingering death by thirst. It wasn't until he saw Merton fetch a length of rope, cut off two conveniently sized pieces and then proceed to tie the injured man's ankles together, that he finally saw that all this was in deadly earnest. He stuttered, 'you c-c-can't do that. It's n-not right!'

Abe Merton looked at the youngster coldly and said, 'You want to free that sister of yours?'

'Of course I do!'

'Then shut your mouth. Go over to your horse and make ready to leave.'

Having bound the man's ankles, Merton finished off by forcing the now helpless man's mouth open and inserting one of the bits of rope. He then tied it at the back of the fellow's head, effectually gagging him, following which he delivered himself of the following words: 'You're like to die here and I ain't a bit sorry. Anybody'd prey on young girls the way you and your friends have done – well, you deserve what comes to you.'

As he mounted up, Abe Merton wondered if his young partner would feel strongly about the plight of the Comanchero to go back and free him. Seemingly he was not concerned to that degree, for he followed on when Merton urged his horse forward.

What Merton was aiming at was to skirt around the hills until he found some path or track leading higher up. Like as not, they'd be obliged to dismount and lead their horses, but that was fine. Knowing that they wouldn't be heading off from their camp this very day gave him time to consider on things and formulate a plan. Ed had said nothing at all since leaving the injured Comanchero to his fate and Merton had an idea that the boy was vexed with him. He said, 'I spoke right sharply back there. I'm sorry.'

'That don't matter. How d'you know that fellow was even mixed up with snatching the girls? Maybe he was just a hanger on.'

Merton shrugged and looked sideways at Ed. He said, 'You ride with an outlaw, you die with an outlaw. There's no more to it than that. You don't have the belly for work like this then you can head back to your ma. You'll recollect that you asked to come along with me. I told you to turn back.'

They rode on in silence. Thinking that he had been too rough, Merton said, 'Listen, boy, if that young cutthroat spoke true then we've twenty men to tackle. That's ten to one against us. Any edge we can get, we take. Don't waste your tears over that worthless dog we left back there.'

'What'll we do when we get up into the hills?'

'I'm not sure yet. Depends on one or two things.

You read scripture?'

'Scripture? Not hardly. My ma made me attend church, but I didn't take to it overmuch.'

'It tells in the book of Judges how Gideon and his men crept into the heart of the Midianite camp at night. They took the place by surprise and the three hundred of them beat an army of thousands. Maybe we'll try that dodge.'

'Sun's only just risen. What are we going to do for the rest o' the day?'

Merton gave a short bark, which might have been taken for a laugh, and said, 'Happen you're sharper than I took you for at first. What we do first is find this camp and see what we can make of it.'

The lower reaches of the hills were covered partly in turf, with scrubby little trees and bushes somehow managing to survive on the rocky ground. Elsewhere was bare, white rock. As Ed had said, this looked to be limestone. Here and there were little streams, which was surprising on a hillside, and which Merton assumed were from some freak geological occurrence. They appeared to spring from the rock and then trickle down to the lower ground.

At length, the two men came to a point where it was clear that the horses would be no further use to them. The trail they were following was along a stony gully that was covered in loose stones, scree that had tumbled down from the frost-damaged rock faces. Even if the horses were able to pick their way through this area, they would make the devil of a noise doing so. By good fortune, a little stream ran along the side of this gully and a bristlecone pine was somehow clinging to life, although the Lord alone knew what nourished it up here. They tethered their mounts to the tree so that they could drink from the stream when the urge took them. Then the two of them made their way up the rugged slope on foot.

After trudging along for a good half hour, disaster almost struck Merton when he found that the pair of them had just attained the crest of one of the hills and below them lay a large, shallow, saucer-shaped indentation; something like a natural amphitheatre. In the middle of this depression, which covered about ten acres, was a hive of activity, with men and horses milling around and the sound of voices. By some fluke, they had not been spotted from below, which was something of a miracle, since they must be outlined against the sky when seen from the camp. For there could be little doubt about it, this was the temporary stronghold of the Comancheros who they were seeking.

As soon as he had figured out the play, Merton dropped to the ground, dragging the boy down with him. Ed said, 'You think they saw us?'

'I'd o' thought that there would have been shouting or shooting, had that been so. No, I don't reckon we were seen.'

'What do we do next?'

'We think. Just hush up for a space, while I take this in and consider on what's to be done.'

It wasn't necessary for Abe Merton to peep over the edge of the crater again; he had seen the entire vista. There had been a makeshift corral full of horses, a few open carts and a bunch of men walking around. Then there were some women and girls too, seated on the ground, keeping themselves separate from the men. Merton hadn't seen if the girls were shackled or bound, but he thought that this would hardly be needful during the day. Anybody trying to sneak away from the camp would soon enough be seen by one or another of the desperados.

Young Ed, who apparently suffered from a constitutional inability to remain silent for more than sixty consecutive seconds, said, 'Well, sir, what next?'

'You stay right down there out of sight. I'm going to scan the scene.'

Very slowly and cautiously, Abe Merton raised his head and crawled forward a few inches until he could see the entire camp spread out before him, maybe fifty feet below. It was just as he had remembered from that first brief glimpse. His eyes ran over the place, looking for an edge, some slight chink in the armour that might be turned to his advantage.

One possibility would be to fire down on the men with the Whitworth. He'd enough ammunition, but the drawback to that scheme was that it was a muzzleloader. At best, he might manage two shots a minute, if you factored in carefully aiming. If those boys down there knew their onions, and he had no doubt that they did, then they would scatter and work their way around the rim of the depression to where he lay. Either that or they'd throw up enough fire so that he would be unable to take proper aim. At best, he might kill one or two that way.

Another idea would be to use the boy at his side as a decoy, setting him off like a hare in the hope that this would take the bulk of the men away from the camp. That would be a scurvy trick to play on the youngster, but Merton's chief concern was his daughter, not some random acquaintance he'd met on the road. Still, that too was not certain. Surely they'd leave enough men to guard the girls, who were worth good cash money to them.

The other option would be to slow those fellows right down and make the job of transporting their captives to the Rio Grande a slow and arduous business. Turning this idea over in his mind and examining it from various angles suggested to Merton that for want of anything better, that was the way to go. He wriggled back down a-ways until he was out of sight once more from the men he was hunting and said, 'How far would you say the town of Endeavour is from the foot of these here hills?'

The boy's brow furrowed as he thought about this and he said tentatively, 'I don't know. Ten or twelve miles?'

'I would say that's about right. I want you to go errands for me in town.'

'You mean to get rid of me? No, don't think it for a moment. I'm staying right here at your side.'

'Listen, you young fool: as matters presently stand, we've not one chance in a thousand of freeing your sister or my daughter. All we'll do is get killed for our pains.' Merton outlined shortly the plans that he had considered and his reasons for rejecting them.

'So what do you have in mind?' asked Ed suspiciously.

'Those boys are aiming to take those women to the border in those carts down there. There must be something approaching a smooth way that they use, a little like a road, I guess, which will lead them down out of these hills and onto the plain. It's what to the border from here, as the crow flies? I should say, from all that I am able to collect, it might be thirty-five miles. Yes?'

'I guess so.'

'If you load those girls into carts and drive the horses hard, you might do three or four miles in an hour. Meaning if they started at first light tomorrow, then they could run for the border and be there inside ten hours. If there was a boat waiting, then by tomorrow night they'd have 'em safe in Mexico. Now if some mischief were to befall those carts and maybe some of the horses were killed too, then you're looking at getting those girls to walk the distance.

You'd be lucky to manage more than two miles in an hour and if you didn't have regular breaks, they'd be fainting and collapsing and I don't know what all else. Agreed?'

'I suppose, but I don't see . . .'

Merton cut in with the greatest irascibility, saying, 'Just listen. There's no chance that they'd get those girls to walk thirty-five miles in one day, not in this heat. You might manage twenty; you couldn't get them to do thirty, let alone thirty-five. That gives us time to get something else happening. I don't know just what yet. Maybe we can reduce the odds a little tonight while we put their wagons out of commission.'

'You promise you won't act till I return? Word of honour?'

'We're not in the schoolyard. I need what I'm asking you to go to town and fetch. I want to stay here and watch further.'

'All right, what do you want me to get?'

'Good man. I want a quart flask of lamp oil, a keg of powder, maybe five pounds weight if you can get it, and some fuse. A box more of Lucifers wouldn't come amiss either. Think you can remember all that?'

'Yes, you've no need to write me a list. It'll take upwards of four, five hours for me to get there and back, you know, even at a trot.'

'Don't race. A steady trot'll do better than a canter.

56

Long as you get back 'fore dusk, we'll do well enough.'

After Ed had gone, Merton removed the heavy musket from his back and detached the telescope that was fastened to the left of the barrel. It wasn't the most powerful spyglass in the world, but would serve him better than his naked eye. Very slowly and carefully, Merton crawled back up until he was able to peer down into the encampment of the Comancheros once more. The sun was behind him, so he did not need to fear being betrayed by the flash of reflected light from the lens of his telescope. He trained it on the camp and examined carefully all that he was able to see.

First off he looked around to see if he could find his daughter. She was sitting among a group of other young women and did not appear to have been harmed. She certainly looked sad – as well she might, given her circumstances. After all, not only had she been stolen away and was being held prisoner, but for all the child knew to the contrary, her father was laying dead. Merton wished that he could send a signal to reassure her that not only was he alive, but that he intended to free her within a short time. It would have been sheer madness though to draw any attention to himself, and so he was content to think of the vengeance he would visit upon the unmanly wretches who had carried her off in this way. As a God-fearing man, Merton was perfectly familiar with the verse of scripture in which the Lord firmly sets His face against private vendetta, saying most clearly, 'Vengeance is mine, saith the Lord; I will repay.' For all that, he did not feel that this was a task that he was able to leave entirely to the Lord, touching as it did upon his child's welfare.

There were eleven girls, including Hannah, and thirteen men that Merton could see. There were no tents and presumably everybody was just sleeping out under the stars, which would present no hardship at this time of year. Then there were the carts, two of them. Casting his eye over them, it seemed to Merton that these were most likely ordinary covered wagons that had been stripped of their canvas hoods. Perhaps these were loot from some previous ambush of peaceful settlers heading west to California. One thing was for sure: these fellows could not have been long in this area, snatching people's sisters, wives and daughters in this way. If that kind of beastliness were happening regularly, then it would not take long for a vigilance committee to be formed to tackle it. No, these men must have just lately come to these parts and be collecting a bunch of girls in a hurry, before dashing across the border.

About half the men whom Merton observed through the telescope were dark skinned: half-breeds, or maybe Mexican or Spanish. The rest looked as pale as Merton himself. It had been a right long while since he had had anything to do with such matters, but he did recall that these Comancheros had a close relationship with both the Kiowa and Comanche. They traded together and helped each other in various ways. Had these men come from the northern part of Texas, where it was rumoured a state of virtual war existed between the Comanche and the army? Maybe the going had become a little too hot for this crew up there and so they had decided to retreat to Mexico, taking with them enough girls to provide them with a little stake money when they had crossed the border.

The hours stretched before Abe Merton, and since nothing seemed to be likely to happen before Ed returned with the supplies, he supposed that he might as well go back to where he had left his horse and have a drink. It would do no harm to check over the rifle that he'd bought, either, just to make sure that it was in good working order.

Ed's horse was gone, of course, but Merton's was standing there patiently. They had not been together long enough to get to know each other, but the creature consented to being caressed and stroked a little. After he had slaked his thirst from the stream, Merton sat down and stripped the Whitworth, checking all the component parts. It all seemed in good order and lacked only a little oiling. The weapon was legendary for its accuracy over great distances, which was what he had mostly used it for during the war when he had fought from time to time as an irregular, harassing

Union forces as they passed near or by Arkansas. He recalled his favourite story of the Whitworth, a number of which had been sold by England to the Confederate army during the war.

At the Battle of Spotsylvania Courthouse in 1864, Union General John Sedgwick had come across some private soldiers dodging and sheltering from Confederate sharpshooters, who were firing from over half a mile away. He had chided them angrily, saying, 'I'm ashamed of you men, hiding like this from a few single bullets. Why, they couldn't hit an elephant at this distance!' At that very moment, the general fell dead with a bullet that entered just below his left eye and blew his skull to atoms. The fatal shot had been delivered by a Whitworth, and Merton had met at least a half-dozen men in the four years since then who had sworn that they alone had fired the shot which killed Sedgwick.

Sighting down the barrel showed Merton that this rifle should fire true and he reassembled the weapon reassured. Then he took the Colt Navy apart and went through the same process of checking every part. If there was to be shooting, he wished to be well assured that neither of his guns was apt to misfire.

CHAPTER 4

It was the better part of six hours and well past noon when Ed returned with the various provisions that Merton had asked him to fetch. He had also, on his own initiative, purchased some more comestibles, for which Abe Merton was mightily grateful. He said, 'That was well thought of, son. We'll make a seasoned campaigner of you yet.'

'You still think we should . . . go for them after dark?'

'That I do.'

'But dusk ain't like to fall for a good eight hours yet. What shall we do till then?'

Abednego Merton looked at the youngster and couldn't help liking what he saw. The boy was so fresh-faced and eager for action. He said slowly, 'When folk talk about wars and fighting and such, they always manage to make it sound like it's one long run of excitement. Well, it ain't. There's a deal

61

more waiting around and getting bored than there is lively action. You might have a week of marching round and sitting doing naught, following by a few hours of shooting and killing. Then it's all quiet again for days, sometimes weeks. It's like to be the same now.'

'So what do we do now?'

'Like I said, we sit and wait.'

Merton was perfectly content to sit and think for a few hours and had no need for anybody else's company while doing so. It was altogether different for Ed, who was unable to sit still and stop fidgeting. At first he sat and shied stones at a nearby rock, until one of them ricocheted off and almost struck Merton, whereupon he requested the youth to desist. For the next few minutes, the young man looked about him restlessly, made humming noises and then, to Merton's horror, began whistling. At that he said sharply, 'Have you lost your senses, boy? You want to advertise our presence here?'

Slowly, the hours crawled by, interspersed with the occasional stretch of desultory conversation and both men sleeping a little. After the sun had set and dusk was approaching, Merton told the young man, 'You wait here. I'll be back directly.' Once more, he detached the telescope from his rifle and made off up the slope. By this time, Ed had seen enough of the older man's ways to know that had he wanted company on his scouting then he would have said.

When he returned, Merton said, 'I wanted to check that the carts are well away from people. I don't reckon that once the trouble erupts that any of those prisoners will feel the urge to fly towards danger.'

'What's your purpose? What will we do?'

'What kind of shot are you with a musket?'

Ed didn't bother to boast, but instead gave the question some thought. After a pause, he said, 'Fair to middling. Good enough for hunting.'

'You never fire a heavy calibre musket?'

'No, sir, mostly scatterguns, you know.'

'But you can load and reload and keep firing in some general direction?'

'I guess.'

Abe Merton set out his plan for the night's adventure, which sounded to Ed almost in the nature of a suicide mission. His own role was less hazardous, but even so, there would be danger enough. As Merton set out the scheme, he would creep after dark into the Comanchero camp. As he said, they would be watching to stop their prisoners' escape, rather than expecting anybody to try and sneak in. Once there, Merton would place the keg of powder on one of the wagons and then drench them both in lamp oil. Then he would fire the wagons and try and slip away unseen in the chaos that would doubtless ensue. Ed's part in the affair would be to keep the Whitworth trained on the camp and, if shooting began, to start firing at anybody near the carts. Merton stipulated this, because he thought that once the fire began then the girls would tend to keep as far away from it as they were able. He did not want to see the youngster shoot one of the captives in error.

'Think you can do it?' asked Abe Merton. 'Just fire a few shots down as a distraction if you hear any shooting?'

'I reckon so.'

'Good fellow. I'll just run over the operation of that musket. The recoil's something else again; you'll need to be sure to keep it pressed firm against your shoulder or it'll come near to breaking your collar bone. You'll feel like you got kicked by a mule.'

They waited for another two hours until it was pitch dark. The night was moonless, which was auspicious. Together, the two of them made their way up the slope. By good fortune, Ed had been able to buy a five-pound keg of powder, which should make for a good explosion if matters proceeded as planned. He cradled this with one arm, while carrying the can of lamp oil in the other hand. Over the lip of the rise, they were able to see the cheerful, ruddy glow of a campfire.

From all that Abdenego Merton was able to see, things could not have been better arranged had he been able to direct the disposition of the bandits to his own satisfaction. There were more men than before, indicating that the other party of which he had been told had now arrived to complete the complement. In the flickering light, he was able to see that the girls were well away from the fire and entirely separate from their captors. The wagons were right on the other side of the camp from the girls; far enough away that nothing that happened there would be likely to harm them. There was always a risk, of course, but if he failed to act, then there was nothing but stark certainty that his little girl would fetch up in a Mexican brothel and, from Merton's point of view, death would be a thousand times preferable to that fate.

Checking that his pistol was securely tucked in his belt and that the knife which he had used to slay the horse earlier that day was safely in the sheath affixed to his belt, he whispered to the lad at his side, 'Mind now, not a shot are you to fire unless either me or one of them starts shooting. Is that plain? And if you do have to fire, make sure you don't aim anywhere near those girls over there, you hear what I tell you?' Then he slipped off into the darkness, leaving a boy of fifteen as his only cover in what promised to be an exceedingly dicey and uncertain business.

Despite having told Ed that he thought that the men in the camp would be more worried about those wishing to escape, rather than fearing anybody approaching by stealth, Merton took careful stock, when once he had circled round the rim of the depression in which the Comancheros had established their base. After making almost a half circuit, all the time treading as lightly as he was able for fear of alerting anybody to his presence, Merton found the smooth track along which they had most likely brought the carts into the hollow that they currently occupied. He peered down through the darkness and saw that a man was sitting on a boulder below him smoking at his leisure. This could only be their lookout of sentry.

Perched as he was, six or ten feet above the man, Merton wondered what his best strategy might be for disposing of him without rousing the rest of the nest of skunks. Sometimes, the most obvious, straightforward and brutal way is the quickest and best. This was just such a case. Setting the keg of powder down carefully, Merton placed next to it the flask of oil. Then he drew the knife from its sheath. He was loath to be parted from the pistol, but did not want to run the risk of losing it in a tussle and so, with some little misgiving, he set that on the rocks. Then, since he had already decided upon his course of action and there was no purpose in delaying the execution of his plans, he leapt onto the man's back.

When you are one moment sitting and smoking, while at the same time musing idly on the charms of a young lady whom you hope to see within a few days and make passionate love to, then the arrival on your back from a height of eight feet of a weight of ten stone or so is liable to knock the breath from you and leave you stunned. This was just the position of the young villain who was guarding the path into the camp. His surprise was destined to be short-lived though, for no sooner had he taken a deep breath, preparing to shout a warning to his friends that there was an intruder, than Abednego Merton had grasped his hair, jerked back his head and, with one strong, scything sweep, all but detached the young man's head from his body.

The sound of blood gushing out from the man he had jumped, which sounded in the darkness like water running from a faucet, was more than sufficient to persuade Merton that here at least was one bandit with whom he would not be contending in the future. A little winded himself from crashing into the man in that way, he nevertheless replaced the knife in its sheath and then clambered up the rocks to retrieve the supplies that he had left up there. Then he climbed down rapidly and made his way to the two carts. The boys sitting round the fire had had their night-vision spoiled by the glare of the flames, and even if one of them had turned round now and stared straight towards Merton as he slinked through the shadows, it is doubtful if he would have been seen.

Merton placed the keg of powder on the first wagon, over which he also poured half the lamp oil. Then he splashed the rest of the oil over the other wagon and then placed the earthenware jar in front of the powder keg. It was now facing the body of men clustered around their fire. Satisfied that all was just as he wanted it, Merton took the box of Lucifers from his pocket and struck one. He set the match to a part of one of the wagons where he had poured the oil. It took a second to catch, but then a pale blue flame began to creep up the wooden side of the cart. It was now time to depart. Without running or making any sharp and sudden movements, Merton strolled briskly back the way he had come and then climbed up again to the ring of rocks surrounding the camp. Then he sat down and watched to see what would develop.

With all the hot, rainless weather of the season, the wood of which the two carts were composed was tinder-dry. By the time that somebody noticed what was amiss, both carts were blazing merrily. There was a cry of alarm and then some of the men ran towards the fire and called on the others to bring water. Those first there took off jackets and hats and began beating at the flames in an effort to extinguish them. This was better than Merton could have hoped for, because in no time a dozen men were clustered around the carts, doing their best to put out the flames. They were having some little success with one of the carts and were gradually getting the better of the flames, when there was a roaring boom, like a clap of thunder near at hand. Hungry flames had reached the powder.

A puff of hot air, not unlike that which one gets

when an oven door is opened, passed over Merton. He smiled grimly, wondering what damage his improvised mine had wrought. When the smoke cleared, he could see eight or ten figures lying on the ground. There was a tumult of shouting, swearing, groaning and cries of agony, all mixed in with the whinnying of some of the horses that had been tethered near the carts. Presumably the explosion had shattered the earthenware flask and, as Merton had planned, the fragments and splinters had all been hurled with the speed of bullets at anybody near at hand. Wanting to get back and assure his young partner that he was unhurt, Merton did not linger to observe his handiwork, but moved lower down the slope and worked his way back to the place where he had left Ed with his musket.

'God almighty,' said the boy, when Merton loomed up out of the darkness, 'I was sure you were dead!'

'Not yet. And spare me your profanity. I'll have the Whitworth back, if you please.'

'I saw the fire and the explosion. Are many hurt?'

'I'd say that at least five are killed. That takes the odds against us down a little. A few horses looked to be injured or killed too.'

'What now?'

Merton said, 'We need to get back to our mounts. I know where their little roadway is and I'm guessing that they'll be heading straight for the border at first light.'

'None o' the girls was hurt, I saw that. My sister, she's there all right, with the others.'

When they reached the little stream where the horses were tethered, Abe Merton wanted only to sleep, but the evening's work was the most exciting thing that Ed had ever seen in his life, and he wasn't about to sleep without talking the business over. He said, 'I weren't a bit scared. Thought I would be, but I never felt any fear at all.'

'Any man says as he doesn't have fear when that kind of action begins, he's either a liar or a mad fool. I hope you ain't the latter, for we have other work to do yet.'

Although Merton could not see it in the dark, Ed blushed hotly at his words. After remaining quiet for a few seconds, he said, in a more subdued voice, 'Well, maybe I was a little frightened, but I could still have fired on them fellows, had there been need.'

Feeling that he had perhaps been a mite harsh on the youngster, Merton said, 'You think I don't have fear? Even at this age? I'm nigh on sixty years of age and I am still nervous when I have to risk myself. Maybe more than when I was young. Old men value their skins more, I guess.'

'You, sir? Truly?'

'Yes, I promise you. It's no bad thing. I've rode with men who had no fear at all, and let me tell you, that was scary in itself! A man who does not fear death will do all manner of crazy things.'

There was silence for a minute or so and Merton got ready to say his prayers, imagining that the two of them were now ready to sleep. But Ed had one last thing on his mind. He said, 'Can I ask you something?'

'Be quick about it, then, for I want to rest, even if you don't.'

'Does it bother you, killing men? You seem right casual about it.'

Merton did not reply for a spell and the young man wondered if he was offended, but at last the older man said slowly, 'It bothers me, son. But like it says in the Good Book, all they that take the sword shall perish with the sword. Matthew, twenty-six, verse fifty-four.' He paused for a few seconds, before continuing, 'Me and my girl were just travelling along, minding our own business, when those boys went for us. So far, I killed maybe a half-dozen of 'em, and if I'm spared I mean to kill them all, every last one. They should've kept to their own selves; they've brought this wrath down on their heads through their actions. But I hope the Lord forgives them all the same. I sure as hell won't.'

Ed could think of no answer to this and so he and the old man laid themselves down and endeavoured to snatch a little sleep before what looked likely to be a particularly trying day.

The pain from his cracked ribs woke Abe Merton long before dawn and he lay awake in the darkness, considering the best step to take this day. It was a great mercy that the Comancheros would now be forced to proceed to the border on foot. True, they might at a pinch hoist the girls onto their saddles and try and move like that, but no horse would be able to carry such a load as two people for long, and certainly not for many miles. Merton tried to cipher out the strength of the party. Arithmetic was not his strong suit and so he had to go over the figures twice to be sure that they were correct.

There had originally been thirteen men and eleven girls in that camp. Then a party of perhaps six men and the same number of girls had arrived some time yesterday, before he staged his assault. That meant nineteen men and seventeen girls. He had, he guessed, killed five of the men, which left fourteen of them, along with the girls. The question was, how many horses remained now? Certainly not enough for all to ride. No, that party would be travelling today and tomorrow at a pace limited by the feeblest and slowest of those girls. There would be plenty of time to harry them and take out more of those bandits.

In the sky over to the east, Merton could see the first, faint glimmering of dawn. He sat up and then prodded the slumbering youth roughly, saying, 'Hey there! 'Stead o' sleeping like a hog, why don't you get up and prepare for a lively day? You ought to take shame, youngster like you, still dreaming the day away while an old fellow like me is already awake.'

'What time is it?'

'Time you was up and doing. Come on, we've business to attend to.'

They broke their fast meagrely on dry bread and a little cheese, washed down with draughts of water from the nearby stream. By the time they had finished, the sky had faded from inky black to the deepest blue imaginable. Merton said, 'We can leave our mounts here. I want to spy out the way that those boys are headed. I'm guessing that they'll be breaking camp as early as can be, for they want to cut and run for the border. After last night's game, they know that somebody's taken agin 'em and they'll be on their guard. What they won't do is delay and try to find us, for it would mean searching every nook and cranny of these hills and gullies.'

Together, Abednego Merton and his young companion walked up the slope towards the scene of the previous night's attack. At Merton's suggestion, they veered off to the right before reaching the ridge overlooking the camp, and then clambered up some rocks until they were on the highest point for some distance. Below, they could see not only the encampment, but also the limestone way, as good as a road, which wound its way down to the south in the direction of the Rio Grande.

From their vantage point, which was perhaps three quarters of a mile from the men and girls below, they had a perfect view of the shallow depression in which the bandits had made their base. Removing the Whitworth from his back, Merton separated the telescope and focused it on the scene below. He was able to count twelve men moving about, ready to break camp, and seventeen girls. There were also three men who were seated and, by the look of them, gravely injured. This was all better than he could have hoped for. He said, 'Odds are shortening, son. Down to six to one now, from all that I am able to collect. Happen we can improve on that though.'

Merton reattached the telescope to the side of the musket's barrel and said, 'Once they're on the move, I doubt they'll want to stop and begin quartering the hills in search of us. They know enemies are at hand by now.'

'What do you intend?'

'Once they're fairly on their way, I'm going to knock another of them over. I'll like enough only have a chance for one, because they'll scatter and dive for cover. One less is one less though.'

'You'd shoot at them unawares?'

'I would. You needn't make out as that's a sneaking act or cowardly, neither. Those men know now that they're fighting us and it's for them to end it, if they don't have the stomach for more bloodshed.'

Ed remained silent, which irritated the older man. He had the distinct impression that the boy was implicitly criticising him. He said, 'I only hope that those boys aren't as ruthless as they could be and feel some loyalty to their comrades.'

'Why's that? How will that help us?'

'If they're real villains, they'll leave their wounded behind. If not, then they'll take them along with them. That means three more horses taken up and also it will slow down the rest. Those men won't be much use in a fight. What with the girls and three wounded men, it'll be like a circus parade as they cross that plain. I'll warrant they don't have enough supplies either, which is one more good thing.'

'I don't see that. They run out of water or food, won't they keep it to themselves and not share it with the girls?'

'I'd say so. Means the girls are likely to be walking slower, fainting and whatnot. It'll all tend to slow things down to a crawl.'

Ed looked at Merton with a look that was a cross between admiration for the clear head and cold logic of the other, tinged with disgust at the almost inhuman calculation that underlay his plans. The old man might well be right about how things worked and his efforts might bring back Ed's sister, but he surely wouldn't like to be such a man in forty years time.

Interpreting the young man's look correctly, Abe Merton sighed and said, 'Think of me what you will. I'd a sight sooner have my daughter safe with me, even if she was a little footsore and hungry, than have her sold into slavery across the border.'

Taking an accurate shot at something in excess of eight hundred and eighty yards is no mean feat, and as he sighted down the telescope, Merton said, 'They're saddling up, ready to leave. You duck down out of sight now. Soon as I shoot, we're going to slip away quietly and fetch the horses.'

'You don't think they'll come up here looking for us?'

'No, I wouldn't say so. They don't have enough men to search all over these hills.'

Laying there watching the bandits mount up and start ordering the girls and getting them to start walking, Merton thought what a fine thing it would be if these boys had a leader of some sort. If they did and he could take out that man, it would make things easier for him and the boy. He observed the scene below him closely. All the men appeared to be equals and no special notice was being taken of one over the rest.

There did not seem to be any spare mounts at all, which meant that Merton's mine must have killed a few of the horses as well as men. This too was heartening, for it meant that those boys had no leeway at all. They could not afford to overburden any of the beasts, which in turn would mean that the girls would not be getting any rides this day. Hannah was tough enough and he didn't suppose for a moment that she would be the first to faint from heat, thirst or exhaustion, but he would be prepared to wager a considerable sum that at least one or two of those young women, maybe more, would collapse before dusk.

All seemed ready now for the departure of the men and their captives. Not seeing anybody who could pass for a leader, Merton thought that the next best thing might be to take down the biggest or most vicious-looking of the men. It was hard to choose between them at this range, so in the end, he chose one of them at random. By good fortune, some of the riders who had not yet begun to move off were bunched together, which meant that if he missed his target, then chances were he'd hit another of the bastards.

Breathing slowly and evenly, Merton drew down on his target. The rifle was resting on the rocks, which meant that it was as steady as you like. All he needed to do was ensure that he did not jerk in the slightest degree when he squeezed the trigger, but he had used this same kind of weapon often enough in the past to make that a remote likelihood. He breathed in, held his breath for a fraction of a second, and then fired. Merton had the immense satisfaction of seeing the man at whom he had been aiming clutch his chest, and then slip sideways, falling off his horse. The odds had shortened a little more.

CHAPTER 5

Just as he had predicted, no attempt was made to hunt for Merton and his partner. They slipped down from the rocks upon which they had been perched and then made their way back down the ridge to where their horses were. As they walked, Ed asked, 'Did you get him?'

'I got him.'

Once they reached the mounts, the two of them tacked up and then paused for a brief while. The youngster said, 'I guess you got a plan. If we show ourselves out in the open, I reckon they'll be on us like a duck on a June bug.'

'I reckon you got that right.'

'So, what's to do?'

'We can't ride against them straight, for they still outnumber us. No point trying to pick 'em off one by one, either. They're wise to that. They know for sure that they got an enemy near at hand and they'll set a watch for us. We ride on at a good distance and see if anything promising turns up.'

Ed said bluntly, 'Does that mean you don't know what we're going to do?'

'That's about the strength of it, son.'

The two men led the horses back down the slope until they were on the north side of the hills again. They would ride along, looking for a pass or something of the kind which might lead through the range of hills and bring them out onto the open land which lay between there and the Rio Grande. Merton wasn't at all worried about losing time in this way; he knew that the Comancheros and the girls they had stolen away would be proceeding at the pace of the slowest of the girls.

Eleven men. This was the only fact that concerned Abe Merton presently: that he needed to bring about the deaths of eleven men. Well, fourteen, if you counted the three men who were wounded, but Merton had hoped that one or more of them might be so grievously injured that they would die of their own accord, without his having to factor them into the equation at all. He supposed that at a pinch, even a wounded man could handle a musket or perhaps affect some harm to the girls, so he couldn't afford to leave those three altogether out of his reckoning.

It took three hours for Merton and the boy to work their way round and find a pass through the hills that led south. The pass, when they came upon it, was so perfect for cutting through the high ground to the plain beyond that Merton was uneasy, thinking that it would be a fine place to set an ambush. He reined in and told Ed to do the same. For a while, he just sat there astride his mount, rubbing his chin thoughtfully. Having weighed up the options available to them, and realizing that in truth they amounted only to pursuing the bandits as they made for the border, Abe Merton jabbed his heels into the horse's flanks and rode forward at a trot.

When the young man had caught up with him, he said to Merton, 'We lost a chunk o' time there, riding round till we found this pass, I mean. Those fellows'll have a right good lead on us.'

'You can make your mind easy as to that,' Merton replied, 'Truth to tell, I'd be surprised if they've properly got going yet. You ever tried to get a young girl to hurry up in the morning? They got more than one to get going.'

'You're sharp with that rifle,' said Ed. 'You said you had one during the war. What unit was you in? Happen you knew my pa.'

'Was your father in a regular regiment?'

'He was in Company K of the first infantry regiment, the "Texas Invincibles", you know.' There was an unmistakable note of pride in the boy's voice as he named the unit in which his late father had served.

'Why then, our paths ain't like to have crossed.'

'You're from Arkansas though. I know my pa's company was up in that neck of the woods.'

Merton made no reply and hoped that the subject was now exhausted, but after a minute or two, Ed said, 'Most all the men I know fought for the Confederacy are proud as you like and tell their regiment straight off. You sound like you're ashamed of being in the army.'

There was another long pause, before Merton spoke again. He figured that it would do no harm to be a little more open with this young man, to whom he was taking something of a liking. He said, 'I reckon I was in the army above twenty years, son. You needn't doubt that I was a soldier.'

'Twenty years? You mean you were in the regular army before the war?'

'Long before then, yes. That was the United States army, mind. No Union or Confederates in those days.'

'But you took part in the War Between the States?'

'In what you might describe as an irregular capacity, I did, yes.'

'You were a guerrilla fighter? But you're. . . .'

'Old?' said Merton, a grim smile twitching at his lips. 'Not too old though to fire a musket, which is how the Whitworth come in handy. I was fighting from a distance, as you might say.'

Ed said nothing, mulling this over. Merton felt that

he was being weighed in the balance and found wanting, that the youngster thought that firing at an enemy from a distance of half a mile or more might not be an honourable way of going about things when compared with riding into battle, as his late father had evidently done. He said slowly, 'I can see where your thoughts are tending, son. Maybe you're thinking there's something sneaky and underhand like about shooting men from a way off?'

The boy shrugged, but gave Merton a sideways look that indicated that this was just precisely what he'd had in mind.

'I lived my whole life long by following the rattlesnake code,' said Merton, 'if you know what that is. I never shot a man unawares, without giving challenge first. How'd that square with my tip-and-run attacks during the war?'

'I wondered.'

'Here's the way of it. If a fight starts and a man is pursuing you with murder on his mind, then he has to look to his defence. Once the fighting's begun, anything is allowed. You can lay ambush or shoot from behind . . . anything you please. That's what it was in the war. The Yankees were fighting us and they had no business coming to Arkansas. We didn't ask 'em to visit. My way of thinking was that this was like when you know somebody's chasing you with murder on his mind. You can do anything you like then to stop him.'

The pass through which they were travelling was flattening out as they came the end of the little range of hills. At some points, limestone cliffs had towered above them on either side, but now there were only gentle slopes covered in scrub. Before them, they could see the open plain that lay, more or less uninterrupted, for thirty miles or more to the Rio Grande. It was time to slow down and take stock. Abe Merton halted his horse and signalled with his hand for his companion to do likewise.

'We'll go forward at a walk,' said Merton, 'But be ready to stop or take flight, back the way we came, at the first sign of trouble.'

'I ain't running!'

'You'll do as I bid you.'

They walked their mounts on slowly, all the while keeping a wary eye on both the plain ahead and the hills to right and left. There was no sign of anybody though. Then, some way away and to the left, Merton caught a glimpse of movement. He froze and held up his hand warningly. There was nothing to fear though, for what he had seen was a group of people perhaps a mile away, making their way across the plain. He and Ed would hardly be visible from here, even if somebody in the party that they were observing should chance to turn their heads and stare straight at them. The sun was shining, but the two riders emerging from the pass were in shadow and unless they began dancing around or performing rodeo tricks, there was little to distinguish them at that distance from their surroundings.

'It's just like I said,' declared Merton, with satisfaction, 'They ain't hardly got going yet. They'll spend at least one night, maybe even two, sleeping rough.'

'What do you say we should do?'

'We're going to do nothing for an hour or so. Let them get a good head start on us. Then we'll ride off to the west, over yonder, and make sure that we're at least two miles from them. Just keep pace.'

'Won't they see us?'

'Don't much mind if they do,' said Merton imperturbably. 'That's the beauty of it, don't you see?'

'How's that, sir?'

'Well now, they can't leave those girls untended, else they'll all run off. It'd be like rounding up cattle to fetch 'em all back again. That means that only a few men would be able to come after us, if they saw us. Odds'd be pretty well equal. Better, since I've the Whitworth and might be able to pick them off before they get close to us. No, if they see us, they won't be coming for us, not unless we get too close.'

'Couldn't you just pick a few more of them off that way, if that rifle's all you say?'

This was the sort of conversation that Abednego Merton enjoyed, or rather had enjoyed when he was a fighting man. He considered the youngster's question for a few seconds before replying and then said, 'You say you've hunted with a scattergun? You'll know then that if you're hoping for to take down a flying bird, you needs must aim ahead of it, for your buckshot or ball will take time to reach the target. Else your bird will have passed the point you're aiming at.'

'Sure, anybody knows that.'

'Well, if it's like that at fifty or a hundred feet, just imagine if your target is a half-mile off. It'll take a ball from this piece of mine two or three seconds to travel a half-mile. Think how far a rider could have moved in that time! Against a stationary thing, nothing beats a Whitworth at distance, but if something's on the move, then you can forget it. It keep still though; why even the queen of England scored a bull's-eye at a quarter of a mile with one o' these.'

'Queen Victoria? How's that?'

'Well, it seems that her majesty was at some big shooting show they hold in England. I don't recollect the name of the competition, but they wanted her to open it with a bang. Rigged up a Whitworth, had it held securely in a vice or some such. All Victoria had to do was tug on a string wound round the trigger. Plumb bang in the bull at four hundred yards. Just before the war.'

The two of them waited until Merton said that it was wise to leave, Ed thinking it was no bad idea to be guided by the older man in matters relating to cunning and crafty fighting. He himself had, after all, no direct experience of such things. When

Merton said it was safe, they trotted off at a diagonal angle from the men they were following, until they found themselves perhaps a mile and a half from the bandits and their prisoners, moving south in parallel to them. Ed said, 'You think they've seen us?'

'I reckon so. Know we're enemies too, I dare say. It's no matter.'

For the rest of the morning, they carried on in that way, keeping their distance from the Comancheros, although making no effort to hide from them. It was probably as Abe Merton had said: they could not leave the girls alone or they would be running every which way to escape.

The pace of travel was, as Merton had predicted, extremely slow. Even when they slowed down their mounts to a leisurely walk, they still found that they were outpacing the others and had to stop for a spell until the bandits and their captives drew level again. By the time that the sun was at its highest point in the heavens, Merton calculated that they had moved no more than five miles from the hills. He said, 'At this rate, they'll be lucky to reach the border this side of Thanksgiving. Were I in their position, I might be thinking about cutting my losses and abandoning those girls out here in the wilderness.'

'You think they might do that?'

'Not really, no. But they're surely going to find this a hard row to hoe.'

'We ain't exactly in the best situation ourselves,'

remarked the young man, 'We've food enough for today perhaps and enough water in our canteens, but what happens when that runs out?'

'You never hear where the Lord sent ravens to feed Elijah in the wilderness? In scripture, you know.'

'You say as we should wait for ravens to bring us food when what we have run out?'

Merton laughed out loud, for the first time since his daughter had been taken, and said, 'I hope to settle this before that happens.'

The day dragged on and the speed at which the Comancheros were travelling became less and less. It was plain that the girls were unable or unwilling to move any more that day and so, long before dusk, the party that they were following halted and appeared to be readying themselves for the night where they were, which was in the middle of nowhere.

At Merton's insistence, he and Ed moved further away from the others until they were standing off about three miles. They ate what little food they had left and washed it down with the last of the water in their canteens. It was not yet completely dark, and because they had not the wherewithal to light a fire, Merton and the boy just sat there on the ground in the gathering gloom. After there had been a long silence, Merton said, 'What's your sister's name?'

'She's called Martha.'

'Describe her to me.'

'Sir?'

'Tell what she looks like, maybe what she was wearing when taken. I need to be able to pick her out.'

'She's short, got black hair, usually in braids. Brown eyes, wears a dress. I can't think of anything else. Why'd you want to know?'

'Because I'm fixing for to go to that camp by myself tonight and see if I can't fetch back my daughter and your sister from them as took them, that's why.'

'It would be madness! If you're right, then they know we're after them. They'll set watch tonight.'

'Whether or no,' said Merton, 'that's what I'm a-fixing for to do.'

Ed knew by now that when the man he had picked up with said that he was going to do a thing, then that is what he would do. There was no more to be said and so he sat there turning over the idea in his mind and wondering if this strange old fellow really might be capable of rescuing his sister from the clutches of those villains. He considered too what role he might play tonight, but Abe Merton squashed any such speculation by saying firmly, as he made preparations for his expedition, 'You just set here son, and guard the horses. I'm going to load the Whitworth and leave it in your keeping.'

'Suppose they catch you?'

'Suppose they don't.'

When the sky was utterly black, Merton started towards the Comanchero camp, armed with his knife and pistol. It was three miles or so to the place, as the crow flies, but that wasn't at all how he was going to play it. The route he was taking would mean walking closer to six or seven miles. There was little enough point in walking in a straight line from where he and the boy had stopped, because the men holding his daughter would surely have realized by now that the men dogging their footsteps meant them harm. If they were expecting any trouble, then that would be the direction they would be looking towards. For this reason, Merton set off due north, meaning to circle his target and approach it from the east. He knew, too, that even in the most ferociously disciplined of armies, sentries tend to doze off at around two in the morning.

The new moon helped enormously, because with only the faint glimmer of starlight to reveal him, Merton was able to get within fifty yards of the camp before he felt it necessary to drop to his knees and begin crawling forward. He could see only vague shadows and silhouettes, and all those that he could make out were either lying down or sitting upright. He guessed that one of these was most likely the man whose job was to act as lookout. It was probable that he had positioned himself comfortably and, leaning against a saddle or something, was now resting in the arms of Morpheus.

It was a fair guess that the girls would all be sleeping a little way off from the men. Since the chief part of their value lay in their virginity, there would be no percentage in putting them at hazard of being interfered with. Merton supposed it likely too that they would be tied together in some way, to prevent them all slipping away singly in the darkness. He was well aware that it would be a dishonourable thing to free only his own daughter, along with Ed's sister, and leave the rest of the girls to their fate. He hadn't yet decided how he would proceed, whether he would cut the bonds of them all or just take the two girls in whom he had an interest and be damned to the rest.

It was not until Abe Merton was within a few yards of the groups of sleeping figures that he saw how difficult his task was likely to be. His assumption had been that either through some sense of what was fitting or, more likely, to ensure that their merchandise arrived in the cathouse in an undamaged condition, that the girls would be sleeping some way from the men. This proved not to be the case. The pale light from the stars was enough to show that the girls were all huddled in a group and that the Comancheros had arranged themselves in a ring around them. The idea was, presumably, that if any of the girls were to somehow free herself and try to slip away, she would need to step over the bodies of the bandits to escape. This was bad enough, but there was worse.

Even from fifty feet away, Merton had been able to hear groaning and occasional cries. He had thought that these were just some man having a bad dream, but now that he was right up close, it was plain that this was not at all what it was. An injured man was rocking to and fro in agony, wholly unable to sleep. There was, from Merton's perspective, a definite sense of being hoist by his own petard, for this was without doubt one of those hurt the previous night by his improvised mine. It was a nuisance, because this man's moans were preventing others from sleeping soundly. As he lay there in the darkness, trying to work out what his next move should be, the man's cried reached a crescendo and drew annoyed protests from some of those trying to sleep.

'Cris'sakes, man!'

'Will you shut up?'

'Folk're tryin' to sleep!'

From all of which, Merton took it that at least three or four of those men were awake and that there was accordingly not the remotest chance of his accomplishing his purpose. Much as he hated to do it, when his daughter was only a few feet from him, this was one of those times when discretion was definitely the better part of valour. It would profit his child nothing were he to be captured himself by these wretches. Having made this resolution, he thought it best to wait for the men who had been disturbed by the groaning and moaning to fall asleep again before making off. This plan was frustrated when somebody sat up, fumbled in his pockets and removed a cigarillo, which he then lit by striking a match. By great ill fortune, this man happened to be looking right in Merton's direction as the match flared into light.

The changing expressions on the Comanchero's face were as good as a play to watch and had the situation been less desperate, Merton might have been entertained by the sight, as bewilderment gave way in turn to slowly dawning realization, only to be followed swiftly by fear. The fellow knew that the one who had blown up the wagons and picked off a few of them from a great distance was now crouched a few feet away from him and that his own life hung in the balance. Before he could cry out, Merton had slipped his knife from its sheath and leapt forward, intent on cutting the man's throat before he could raise the alarm. Had the rest of the camp been slumbering deeply, there was just the shadow of a chance that Merton might have been able to kill the man who was about to cry out a warning and then to make his escape without anybody being any the wiser. Unfortunately, not only the wounded man, but also several of those he had disturbed by his complaints were awake. The light from the Lucifer, combined with a sudden flurry of movement alerted them to the fact that something uncommon was taking place. Two or three of them jumped to their feet and went for their weapons, fearing that an attack was under way.

The object of Merton's assault might have been a little slow on the uptake when it came to thought, but having realized that an enemy was at hand, he reacted with the rapidity of a startled cat, whirling to one side as Merton slashed at his neck with his hunting knife. It was a close thing though, so close that the tip of the blade actually sliced through the skin of the fellow's throat. It was no more than a scratch and as Abe Merton lurched past him, falling upon one of the girls, two men leapt forward and disarmed him. Merton knew that he had failed utterly and abjectly.

It took no time at all for everybody in the vicinity to be awakened and start asking what the hell was going on. The noise from the man whom Merton had injured the previous night had ensured that most everybody in earshot had been sleeping only fitfully and waking every hour or so in any case. Somebody had a bull's-eye lantern, which was lit, and the narrow beam shone upon Abe Merton. A few of the men recognized him as the one who had killed their friend when they had ambushed the wagon in which Merton and his daughter had been travelling. It was a delicate situation in which to find himself and Merton could not help but contemplate the possibility of his death coming very soon. In itself, that was nothing. He was right with the Lord and had no fear of facing the final judgement. That he had been unable to rescue his daughter, though, and the thought of the fate that now awaited her for certain-sure, was like a dagger through his heart.

'I know this bastard,' said one of the men, 'You 'member that wagon we knocked over a day or two back? He killed Raul and I made sure we'd done for him as well. Seems not.'

There was a sharp, metallic click as one of the others cocked his piece, saying, 'We can fix that soon enough.'

Another of the men threw out his arm at the very moment that the trigger of the pistol was pulled, spoiling the aim and causing the ball to fly into the sky, instead of through Abednego Merton's breast. The sound of the shot roused those girls who had not yet been awakened by the hubbub of the discovery of an enemy near at hand. One of those who had still been sleeping soundly was Merton's daughter, Hannah. She awoke with a start and looked around her in a daze. She had been dreaming that she was back home in Fort Smith and suddenly coming to in this way, laying on the bare earth in the open air, caused her to be confused for a second or two, until she recollected the true state of affairs and her heart sank like a stone.

Hannah Merton looked over towards where the action appeared to be taking place and suddenly felt an enormous surge of relief sweep over her, which was almost immediately engulfed beneath a wave of despair. She had been convinced that her father had been killed during the raid on their wagon and ever since had surrendered herself to grief. Now, she had both found that her father was, against all expectation, alive but that he was probably about to be killed in front of her.

The man who had prevented Abe Merton from being shot out of hand strode over to where the new prisoner was being held. He did not bother to speak, but instead swung a meaty fist into Merton's mouth, causing two teeth to come loose. Then he said, 'I don't want this son of a whore to die quickly. He's caused us too much trouble for that mercy. Bind him securely and painfully. We'll think in the morning what to do with him. But whatever it is, we all want it to be as slow as possible.'

CHAPTER 6

Ed Cherwell had not fallen asleep following the
departure of the man whom he now thought of as his
partner. He didn't even try, just sat huddled on the
ground, waiting to see what would happen. He had
been sitting like that, as immobile as an Indian, for a
little over two hours when he heard the shot. It came
from the direction of the bandits' camp and when he
looked over that way, he could see a gleam of light, as
though somebody had a dark lantern of something
of that sort. He stared in dismay. It was obvious that
something was amiss and that Merton was either
dead or taken prisoner.

Ed had enough confidence in the old man that he
didn't think for a moment that his own presence
would be betrayed to the Comancheros. He'd a sus-
picion that Merton would die under torture before
giving any information. Which meant, he thought
with a chill, that the entire weight of this enterprise

now rested upon his own shoulders. This was such a heavy responsibility that for a moment Ed felt stifled and almost unable to breathe. Then he recalled the sound of his sister's laughter and saw, almost as clearly as though she had been there before him, her smiling and innocent face. He would achieve this not for himself, but for Martha.

There was no point in moving much before dawn, that much seemed clear. When he did set off, he would only need the one horse too. All the reasons that Merton had set out to him for the bandits not riding after him still held good. It would do no harm for him to be a little further off though while he was shadowing them, but that too could wait until first light. He had his own pistol and also that famous musket which Merton set such a store by. There was no food, but that couldn't be helped. It didn't strike Ed as being a smart move to fall asleep now and so he resigned himself to sitting there cold and nervous for the rest of the night, his eyes straining into the darkness for any sign of a foe creeping up on him.

The night dragged wearily past. Nobody on that stretch of the plain was able to sleep well. The man who had been wounded when the keg of powder exploded was wailing and bemoaning his fate, assuming quite correctly that his hours on this earth were numbered. He had been raised a Catholic, although it was years since he'd been near the confessional. Nevertheless, he remembered enough of the church's teaching to be mortally afraid of dying and being cast down into hell. His groans of agony were now being interspersed with prayers for forgiveness and pleas for help from the deity. 'Lord, I been a sinner, but I'm truly sorry,' he cried aloud. 'Forgive me, Mother of God. Pray for me now and at the hour of my death. I ain't ready for to die yet.' It was a great relief to everybody when this man died an hour before dawn, but by then it was almost time to get moving and so there was little point in attempting to get back to sleep.

Abednego Merton had been tied so hard that the circulation was being impeded in his ankles and wrists. 'They don't unfasten me soon,' he thought with a surprising flash of humour, 'I'm apt to died of the gangrene before they dream up anything worse for me.' He thought of Hannah and hoped that some miracle would save her, but despite his fervent but silent prayers, he didn't see how this was to be done.

As for Hannah Merton herself, her despair had given way to a determination that she would no longer be treated like some head of cattle being herded along towards the slaughterhouse. The girls had discussed things among themselves and pretty much worked out what the game was. The oldest of them was nineteen and the youngest twelve, but all now knew that they were going to be sold into virtual slavery in Mexico. Most of the girls were resigned to what was coming soon, but there were two others besides Hannah who had decided that, come what may, they were not going to end up in a brothel. The only weapon they had between the three of them was a knife that one of them had been using to peel potatoes when she was caught, and had somehow managed to secrete in her clothing. As Hannah saw it, their only chance would be to steal weapons from the guards, although this might end up in somebody being shot. She was a virtuous and religious girl, though, and felt that being killed would be greatly preferable to ending up as a whore.

At dawn, the Comancheros set about rousing the camp with a view to leaving at once. They too were running low on food, which didn't sweeten anybody's temper. Some of the girls had begun to cry as soon as they were ordered to stand up and prepare to move out, asking what there was to eat and expressing their views on the impossibility of marching on an empty stomach. One of the men cuffed a girl round the face with the back of his hand, as an encouragement to stop whining, provoking a furious shout from another of the men, who was worried about any of the girls being marked or disfigured. 'Five hundred dollars apiece, intact and in good condition, you stupid peasant,' he shouted. 'I don't want to see none o' them girls with black eyes and missing teeth, you hear what I tell you?'

Abe Merton, who had somehow contrived to sit

upright, despite his bonds, said to the man who had struck the girl, 'You're a brave one, I don't think! Why'nt you untie me and try hitting me round the face, see what you get in return?' The man ignored him.

When it was time to go, two men came over to Merton and beat him up methodically. The cracked rib took a couple of kicks, which almost made him faint with the pain, and another tooth was dislodged. Merton could feel it with his tongue, surprisingly smooth, and feeling much bigger than usual, due to its unusual position in his mouth. After knocking him about enough to inflict pain, but not to the extent that he might be in danger of passing out, one of the men cut the ropes that secured his ankles and wrists, and hauled him to his feet. Even worse than the pain from the cracked rib was the sudden surge of blood into his hands and feet, now that the constricting ropes were removed.

Merton was marched over to where a big, florid man was impressing upon the girls that they had best not complain or cause any delays today. When he saw Merton, he broke off and turned to him. He said, 'Ah, it is our guerrilla. The man who shoots at us from afar and sneaks into our camp to set off his bomb.'

There was the faintest trace of an accent, although Merton could not quite place it. Either French or Spanish was his best guess, with the latter being the most likely since these men probably moved back and forth to Mexico regularly. At any rate, the English was flawless and grammatically correct, even pedantic. Wherever he hailed from, this fellow had spent most of his life in the United States, or perhaps England.

'I have a little wager with one of my compadres,' continued the man. 'It is to this effect: how long will an old man be able to walk without water or food, and what will become of him when he cannot walk any further? It is a curious bet, no?'

Merton shrugged and replied, 'You're going to kill me. You might as well get on with it. I ain't affeared of any a one of you.'

'No, I don't believe that you are,' said the Comanchero, staring hard at Merton, as though something about him was puzzling. 'So you are ready to die?'

The man before him gave a twisted grin, which showed the loss of a front tooth and said, 'One of us will die. You sure it'll be me?'

Without saying another word, the man turned and left Merton, who had the faint satisfaction of having seen a look of uncertainty and superstitious dread in the other's face. Why he hadn't just pulled his pistol and shot him down like a dog was something of a mystery to Abe Merton, but he had known similar men over the years when he was in the army. Such men were like cats playing with a mouse before they finally despatched it. They gained some unholy joy from tormenting their victims first and demonstrating how completely somebody was in their power. It was only when they had reduced a man or woman to a state of complete helplessness that they would consent to kill them. Mayhap this man expected him at some point to beg for mercy or forgiveness? Well, he'd wait a long while for that.

A man came over with two lengths of rope. These were tied, one to each of Merton's wrists, and he was dragged over to where two riders sat on their horses about twenty feet apart. Without a word, one of the men holding him paid out the rope on his side and walked over to the rider on the left. The rope was then lashed to the saddle of this horse. A similar process was undertaken with the rider to the right. It looked to Merton as though the whole thing was practised and that the men had done something of the sort in the past. The lengths of rope were both of the same size, as though cut for this purpose, and when he glanced down at his wrists he saw with disgust that the rope securing his left wrist was stained with blood. He had no more time to consider the matter, because both riders suddenly spurred on their mounts and Merton found himself jerked off his feet and dragged facedown along the stony ground for a short way.

With his arms stretched out, almost being jerked out of their sockets, there was no way of getting to his feet and the only way that Merton could protect his face from injury was to twist his head to one side. Even so, when the horses came to a halt after a few feet, one side of Merton's face was grazed and bloody. He had been lucky that he had not been drawn over one of the rocks that studded this part of the plain, otherwise his brains might have been dashed out. But these fellows seemingly knew their business too well to let the fun end so early. One of the riders called, 'Get up. We've a long journey ahead of us.' Slowly and with some difficulty, Abe Merton got to his feet and prepared for what promised to be one of the hardest days of his life. So excruciating was the pain in his ribs that Merton could scarcely breathe, but he was still alive, against all expectations. And while there was life, he had always heard, there was hope.

Through the telescope of the Whitworth, Ed Cherwell watched the old man being dragged along and wondered if they meant to kill him at once, but this proved not to be the case. He saw the riders stop and his partner was suffered to get to his feet. While the rest of the people in the camp were standing still, the men enjoying the show, Ed toyed with the idea of putting the telescope back on the side of the musket and chancing a shot at one of the Comancheros. He dared not risk it, though, for if his aim was just a little off there was a very real possibility that he might hit one of the girls instead. Heaven forbid, he might even kill Martha. No, he would have to pursue the plan that he and Abe Merton had previously agreed, of just riding alongside and seeing what might happen.

Hannah Merton watched her father stand up and almost wept when she saw how one side of his face was all over blood. What strengthened her was that there was no sign of despair or weakness in her pa's expression. He stood there like an old oak tree; perfectly self-sufficient and not much bothered, to look at his face, by what was going on around him. Seeing his fortitude under such trying circumstances served to stiffen her own resolve and prepare to fight for both her own and his freedom.

The Comancheros and the girls they had seized set off south, without eating or drinking anything first. They were destined to be on exceedingly short commons until the border was reached, and the decision had been made to delay breaking their fast until mid-morning and they had made a little progress on their journey. Merton walked along with his arms stretched out on either side by the ropes. The riders, to whose saddles he was attached, took care to keep far enough apart that there was a constant, if slight strain, upon his shoulders. At times, he felt as though his arms might be about to be jerked from their sockets. Although he had no intention of begging for mercy, it was beginning to dawn on Abe Merton that there might come a time that day when death would come as a blessed release.

Hannah said in a low tone to the girl trudging along wearily at her side, 'You still got your knife, Sarah?'

'Surely. What's your intention?'

'I aim for to snatch a gun from one of those men and see if we can't make a fight of it.'

'You know how to use a pistol?'

In spite of the grim conditions under which they were labouring, a smile came to Hannah's lips and she said, 'My pa taught me. He always said that a woman never knew when she might be called upon to fight, same as a man. I guess he was right and that the time's arrived.'

The girls were not tied together when on the march. It might be possible for one of them to bolt and make off across the flat plain, but a mounted man would soon be able to ride her down. The chief thing that the men guarding them sought now was speed. They were keenly aware that the US Cavalry were somewhere in the vicinity, on account of the Indian risings, and had no desire to try conclusions with the army. There had been times since the end of the war when army patrols had come across slavers and, after freeing their captives, had hanged all the men engaged in that vile trafficking of women without troubling themselves with the formality of a trial. These were lawless times in the southern part of Texas and courthouses were few and far between.

The girl walking behind Hannah and Sarah was also minded to make a fight of it and was in their counsels. She took a hand in the conversation, saying, 'Don't do nothing 'cept after warning us, you know Hannah. I'll be in on this. I'll be revenged upon those bastards if I die in the attempt.'

Both Hannah and Sarah were shocked at such strong language coming from a girl no older than they themselves. They were both able to excuse it, though, on account of Susan Miles' father and brother had both been killed when she was snatched. Not only that, but she was a different class from them. Both Hannah and Sarah came from respectable, hardworking backgrounds. Susan, though, was what would in other parts of the country have been called a 'cracker' or even 'poor white'. How they recognized this fine distinction, neither of them would have been able to explain clearly, but there it was. Not that it made any difference in the straits in which they currently all found themselves.

'Nobody'll start anything without you,' Hannah assured the other girl. 'It would be madness were we not all to act together.'

'You want to save your pa, we best not delay too long,' observed Susan, 'He ain't too young and I don't see him lasting much longer at this rate.'

The three of them cast their gazes across to where Abednego Merton was walking slowly between the two horsemen. Hannah said, 'Pa's a sight stronger

106

than you'd think, never mind how old he is.'

'You think that other, the fellow who's tracking us, he's like to be any help?' asked Sarah. 'The men, they're not easy about him, you can tell, way they keep looking over to where they last seen him.'

Hannah said, 'I couldn't say. I reckon this is a time when we can't wait on anybody, but have to act for ourselves, else we'll all be locked up in a Mexican house of ill repute 'fore we know it.'

A couple of miles away from Hannah, Sarah and Susan, young Ed was walking his horse along. He had turned loose Merton's mount, because he couldn't see what use an extra horse was in these circumstances. He had also come to a decision: just walking alongside those men and their prisoners in this way was not likely to do anybody any use. He would have to act. Ed had listened well to what Merton had told him of the disadvantage of the Whitworth at too great a distance and knew that the older man was quite right. Well then, he'd simply have to draw his targets closer and ensure that they were not weaving and bobbing about either. The rifle was loaded and he was confident of being able to reload it in less than thirty seconds.

So it was that Ed Cherwell began heading in a diagonal path, slowly decreasing the distance between him and the Comancheros. He wasn't about to try a shot on horseback, so it would be a question of leaping from the saddle as soon as there was any sign of anybody heading towards him. As Merton had said, it was not in reason that a whole bunch of them would come after a lone rider and leave those girls untended. No, the most likely course would be for two or three to come racing down upon him. For this, he needed to be able to vault from his mount and lay on the ground in an instant. His heart was pounding at the thought and his mouth felt coppery and dry. He had never even drawn down on another person, much less fired on them. He didn't even know if he was capable of such an act, but if not then his life span was probably to be measured in minutes rather than years, because as he watched, two men detached themselves from the main body and came riding towards him at a canter.

'What d'ye suppose is afoot?' said Sarah, as she and Hannah watched two of the men guarding them engage in a brief conference with the others and then go haring off across the open ground. 'They look to be in a hurry.'

Hannah was feeling more frightened than she ever had done in the whole course of her life, and when she spoke her voice sounded strange in her ears. She said, 'I don't think as we're like to get a better chance than this.'

'You want to go for those fellows now?' asked Sarah, 'You sure 'bout this?'

'No, but I reckon as we should do it all the same.'

'Susan,' said Sarah, 'You with us when we go?'

'I was born ready,' replied the other girl. 'We don't do something soon, we'll be too weak from hunger to try anything.'

Abednego Merton had been praying as hard as he knew how, but somehow he could not feel the presence of the Lord as strongly as he sometimes did. Still and all, he could hardly expect the Lord of Hosts to send a seraph with a flaming sword just to free the least of his servants from the pickle into which he had got himself. This looked to Merton like one of those occasions when the Lord would help those who helped themselves. He too had observed the two riders head off west and guessed that young Ed had something preparing. The boy had certainly waited long enough to make his move and now all that remained was to ensure that he, Abednego Merton, was ready to spring into action as soon as needed. Perhaps the case was not as hopeless as he had supposed, and that with a little luck, combined of course with the favour of the Lord, he might yet find himself escaping these toils.

As soon as he saw two riders peel off from the rest, Ed jumped down and lay flat on the ground. He had nothing to rest his piece on, and at that sort of range he knew that even the slightest wobble would cause the ball to fly wide. Gazing down the little telescope showed him that, just as he had hoped, the men were heading straight towards him. Had they have been minded to circle round or jink from side to side, then Lord knows what he would have done. As it was, the only change in his targets was that they were growing larger by the second. He cocked the hammer and then tried to slow his breathing, so that it would not cause him to jerk the trigger, rather than just squeezing it gently. He aimed to take the first of the horseman at half a mile and the second as soon after that as was humanly possible.

The two men riding down on Ed Cherwell were brothers, and what one did the other invariably did too. They were a pair of scoundrels, but not the worst of men by a long chalk. Indeed, although they were game for anything in the robbery and rapine line, they were both uneasy about this women business. They had made an effort to ensure that conditions for the girls with whom they were travelling were comfortable, and had spoken privately together and expressed their distaste at work of this kind. They were happier robbing banks or ambushing lone travellers and taking their belongings from them. One was called Jacques and the other Gerard, and they hailed originally from a Creole family in New Orleans.

When the suggestion was made that somebody should go out and tackle the watcher who was now getting closer to their column than was comfortable, Jacques and Gerard had thought that it might be a lark to go out and see if they were faster and tougher than the man who was causing everybody to feel a little nervous about his intentions.

The two young men set off at a canter, feeling that they would be more than a match for any lone rider, whatever his goal. Truth to tell, they half thought that they might be able to rough up whoever it was and maybe both drive him away and gain a little profit from robbing him at the same time. They were about seven hundred yards from the man, who appeared to have taken a tumble from his horse. Leastways, they could see the horse standing there patiently and the rider laying flat on the ground. Jacques laughed and turned to his brother, just in time to see a heavy calibre bullet enter Gerard's right eye, passing straight through his head before emerging at the back in a gout of blood and brain matter. This was all so unlooked for that Jacques simply sat there for a few seconds, trying to make sense of what he had just witnessed, as his brother slumped sideways and fell from his horse. It was a fatal delay.

When the full horror of the thing sank in, Jacques gave a howl of grief and anger and jabbed his spurs viciously into the flanks of the beast he was riding. Mad with fury, he galloped straight at the prone figure lying near his horse. It was the worst possible course of action that he could have taken, for Ed Cherwell had reloaded by that time, and when the second rider was still a hundred yards from him, he fired again. The ball took Jacques in the chest and he jerked back. His horse veered to one side, whinnying in terror and Ed realized to his utter amazement that he had killed both of the men who were coming towards him. Almost without thinking, he reloaded the Whitworth and then went back to his horse and mounted up.

The first shot rolled across the plain like distant thunder, and the three girls who had been planning to attack the men near them went into action with their hearts in their mouths. Like young Ed, Sarah had never in her life launched a deadly assault on anybody, but she knew too that the time was now or never. She walked meekly up to one of the riders and, without hesitating, sank her little knife into his thigh. She withdrew it at once and then reached up and plucked the pistol from his holster. Seeing this, Hannah was encouraged to rush at one of the riders who had her father tethered like a beast. This man was looking around him, trying to make out what the hell was going on and what the meaning could be of those distant shots. He had no apprehension of danger as the young girl came up to him, grabbed the revolver from where it hung at his hip and then fired twice at him.

Seeing what was happening, Merton hardly knew whether to be pleased or horrified. He had already worked out easily enough that the crash of gunfire over to the west was the work of the boy he'd been riding with. When he saw his own daughter run up to one of the horsemen and make a grab for his gun, though, Merton nearly died of shock. He wanted to shout out to Hannah and tell her not to do it, but it was all over before he had a chance; almost as soon as she had the gun, Hannah had used it with deadly effect, hitting the man from whom she had taken it. At the same moment, he heard another shot near at hand and knew that for good or ill, the fight was on for mastery over the Comancheros. The horse of the man whom Hannah had shot tried to bolt, and Merton feared that he would be torn asunder between the two animals, but to his astonishment Hannah was now firing again. This time, her target was the other rider, to whose saddle Merton's left arm was attached. Whether by intention or sheer chance, the first of the girl's shots in that direction hit the horse, which then fell to its knees in distress. Three more shots finished the rider too. His lessons to the child on marksmanships had, it appeared, been to some effect.

The shooting that had erupted near the bandits convinced Ed that it was a case of now or never. He could hardly leave Martha there with bullets flying around. That being so, he slung the rifle over his shoulder, pulled his pistol and then, holding the reins in his left hand, urged on the horse, squeezing it as hard as could be with his knees and heels in order to get every last bit of speed from her. A cloud of blue smoke was drifting over the group of men and girls and there were more shots. He surely hoped that he would be in time to save his beloved baby sister from whatever was happening there.

Susan did not need any knife or gun. She had grown up the only girl among a half-dozen boys and was wont to wrestle with all comers just as well as any of her brothers. When Hannah Merton fired the first shot, Susan launched herself at one of the men on horseback, hauling herself up like a cat. So taken aback was the man that he didn't realize his peril until the girl's hands reached up to his face and clawed at his eyes. This was no token attack or warning; Susan was quite in earnest about gouging out the man's eyes. She dug her fingers into the eye sockets and had the satisfaction of hearing this big, tough fellow scream like a little girl.

Sarah, intoxicated by the sound of firing and the screams of the man whose eyes were being damaged, pointed the pistol at the man from whom she had taken it. She pulled and pulled at the trigger, but nothing happened. Then it dawned on her that she needed to cock the hammer first, which was no easy task. The man from whom she had taken the piece looked as though he was frozen with horror. These men would have been able to put up a stout resistance to any external assault from the army or vigilance men, but the fact that it was a bunch of young girls going for them seemed to have thrown them into confusion. Having cocked the pistol, Sarah fired it straight at the man in front of her and was

114

pleased to see that she hit him right in the belly.

Merton called frantically to his daughter to find a knife and cut his bonds, for he could see that it would not take the Comancheros long before they recovered their wits and began fighting back. As Hannah hurried over with a Bowie knife that one of the men she had shot had carried on his belt, Merton could see that the boy he'd picked up with was riding hell for leather towards them, firing his pistol as he came. It would be a miracle if he didn't hit one of the girls, thought Merton. He snatched the knife from his daughter and slashed through the ropes, without fiddling around cutting the rope right off his wrists. He dropped the knife and dived to the fallen horse, where he could see a carbine nestling in a scabbard at the front of the saddle. Thankfully, it was loaded, and he worked a cartridge into the breech and began scanning the field of battle for a target.

Things were moving too fast for Ed to feel anything other than a weird exhilaration as he galloped down on the bandits and their captives. He was marking his targets as well as he was able, riding hard and not firing randomly, as Abe Merton had feared. Somebody was shooting back, because a ball droned right past his head, buzzing like an angry insect. He saw one man fall and then, to his astonishment, three or four of the bandits galloped off, abandoning the girls. Absurdly pleased, the youngster thought at first that his own actions had been solely responsible for what had happened. He knew nothing of what the girls had been up to, or of the part that Abe Merton had played.

In the end, six of the previously uninjured bandits were dead and the one whose eyes Susan had damaged was no longer able to cause any harm. The three surviving members of the band had turned tail and run. It was a complete rout and none of the girls had been harmed at all. It seemed to Abe Merton and Ed that they had succeeded beyond their wildest dreams and achieved all that they had set out to undertake, and a good deal more besides.

CHAPTER 7

Abe Merton had seen a lot of fighting and martial activity in his time, but he freely admitted that he had never known anything to match this: a bunch of girls and a young boy had somehow defeated a ruthless bunch of Comancheros. Still and all, there it was. He clung to his daughter with whom, against all hope, he was now reunited. Even while he did so, Merton kept an eye on the horizon. There were still three of those devils on the loose and he would not put it past them to try and wreak vengeance on them all for what had happened.

Hannah would not let go of her father, even as he walked around, assessing the casualties and thinking furiously on what was to be done next. Ed Cherwell's sister, likewise, would not leave his side. The other girls sat around. Most of them wore dazed expressions; it was perhaps a novelty for them to be caught up in the middle of fierce gun battle, and the experience – coming hard on the heels of being snatched away from their families – was alarming.

Ed had killed two men with the Whitworth and another as he rode down on the Comancheros. Hannah had also accounted for two men and her friend Sarah had shot one man who was now groaning, having been searched and disarmed by Merton, who had taken the precaution of lashing the man's hands together. Merton himself had taken out another man with the carbine while sheltering behind the carcass of the horse that Hannah had shot. He, too, was dead. This left them with four wounded prisoners in addition to their other problems.

At first, when the heat of battle was still burning within him, Abednego Merton had remembered the promise that he had made in his prayers: he would hunt down and kill every one of those men with his own hands. Once the three survivors had fled, he had stalked over to the injured men and been strongly minded to shoot them all. It was when he stood over the one whose eyes had been all but torn out by the girl who had attacked him that Merton knew that he could not just kill these helpless men. This was despite the urging of the girl who had scratched and mutilated the Comanchero's face. She came over to where Merton was standing and weighing up his options and said, 'This'un, he's like the leader. You don't have the belly to kill him? Then give me your gun and I'll do it my own self.'

'I've yet to make up my mind on it,' said Merton. 'It's a fearful thing to take a life.'

'It's a fearful thing to take a body from her family, after killin' of 'em. Hand me your piece and I'll settle with him.'

The man whose fate they were discussing was a big, fleshy individual and Merton recognized him as the one who had decided that he would be pulled along between the two horses. He said, 'I've no cause to love him, but I won't have him killed. Nor the others, neither.'

The girl looked at him curiously and said, 'You don't look the soft kind.'

'Shooting a man in battle's different from shooting him afterwards.'

Susan walked off, back to where the other girls were sitting and waiting to see what would happen next.

The man who had been injured by the keg of powder was in pain and by the look of his wounds, which were inflamed and oozing pus, he was likely to die of blood poisoning if he didn't receive immediate medical aid. The other injured party was the man whose gun Sarah had snatched and used upon him. Merton didn't think that he had long at all, for the ball looked to have passed through his lung. He was as pale as a ghost and lying on the ground, breathing rapidly and shallowly. Merton squatted down beside him and said, 'From the look of that wound, you ain't going to recover. You want I should pray with you?' The fellow looked at him in disgust and muttered an obscene oath. Merton stood up and said, 'You want to go to meet your maker with curse words on your lips. I guess that's your affair.'

Ed Cherwell was, after his baptism of fire, as eager for praise as a young puppy. Merton duly complied by congratulating the boy on his marksmanship and courage. Truth to tell, he was genuinely impressed by the fact that this green youth had managed to kill three men and emerge without so much as a scratch to show for it, which was, to Abe Merton's way of thinking, no common achievement for a lad of such tender years. Ed asked why the three remaining members of the Comanchero band had cut and run. Merton said, 'If some enemy had been riding down on them, I'll warrant that those boys would have stood fast and fought to the death. They'd seen those girls going for the guns though and you'll recollect there were seventeen of them. Think if they'd all got guns and began shooting! What with that and you coming on at a gallop and firing as you came, and me banging away with that carbine, they hardly knew what to make of it. I guess those last three didn't see where they were going to be able to get all those girls across the Rio Grande and just couldn't see that the game was worth the candle anymore.'

'You reckon as they'll be back?'

'I surely hope not.'

Ed, whose sister Martha was still clinging to his arm like a shipwrecked sailor who had lately been rescued, said, 'What do you propose now, sir? There's precious little food and water.'

'We can get by without food for a time; it's water that's vital, especially in this weather. We'll head back to those hills where we came from. There's streams there to slake our thirst. After that, we'll see.' By which Ed Cherwell understood that the older man had no present notion how to proceed, once they had retraced their steps to the hills.

Merton told Hannah to speak to the other girls and tell them what was planned. He himself went over to the four Comancheros, who were a pitiful sight. The one who had been shot through the lung was clearly on his last legs, for his breathing was feeble and a clammy sweat had broken out on his brow. If he lasted another half-hour, Abe Merton for one would be remarkably surprised. The two who had been injured by his bomb were sitting listlessly, knowing that whatever happened now, their days were most likely numbered. Either they would die of their wounds, or the grim old man who seemed to have charge of the situation would probably hand them over to the law, which meant hanging for sure. It was to the fourth of the group that Merton went, squatting down beside the man who was almost certainly now stone blind.

'Are you able to see in the slightest?' asked Merton, 'Or will somebody have to lead you?' He could not bring himself to look closely at the man's ravaged face, with the eye-sockets all over blood.

'Can't see a thing. That damned wildcat tore me up good.'

'We're leaving soon. I'll trail a rope from one o' the mounts, which you can hold, so you don't go astray.'

The man who had condemned Abe Merton to what looked to be a long and hard death was now minded to seek his pity, for he said, 'You have no mercy in your heart?'

'I got mercy,' replied Merton, 'I ain't shot you, have I? You set off down a road as isn't likely to do you or anybody else good; what d'you expect? Says in scripture, "Whosoever rolleth a stone, it shall return upon him." I reckon that just about fits the case here.' With these comforting words, he stood up and continued to make the necessary arrangements for moving everybody to the hills where, at the very least, they would be able to drink their fill of fresh water.

The others, including his own daughter of course, were evidently looking to Abe Merton for salvation and so he considered what the next step should be. There were ten horses, which meant that the girls would at least be able to ride for some of the time, taking turns. This should speed up their journey back to the town of Endeavour. Perhaps he could send Ed to the town to fetch help and supplies. Before setting off, Merton told everybody to root through the packs and saddle-bags of the Comancheros and see what there might be of use.

There was hardly any cash money among the belongings of the bandits. The only useful thing to be found was the meagre supply of food. At a pinch, this looked as though it might provide two very skimpy and inadequate meals. Since none of them had yet eaten so much as a morsel that day and they faced a long journey, Merton directed that the food should be divided in half and that everybody should have a meal before they started out. 'Meal' was perhaps being overly generous to the provisions upon which they broke their fast that morning. It amounted to a couple of mouthfuls of stale bread and a little cheese, and some wind-dried beef that was as tough as leather.

While the girls were eating, Merton called Ed Cherwell aside for a brief conference. He said, 'What would you say to you riding hell for leather to town and raising the alarm? Fetching help out here, I mean.'

'And leave my sister? I don't think it for a moment.'

'That's what I thought you'd say,' admitted Merton, 'but it would make our task a sight easier were you to do it.'

123

'Well, I won't and that's flat,' said the boy, 'Comes to that, why don't you leave your daughter out here and make the journey yourself?' Seeing the look on the older man's face, Ed continued, 'No, I didn't think you'd take to that scheme. We're in the same case. Neither of us'll even think of it.'

Merton sighed and said, 'Happen you're right. Well then, soon as we've finished eating, we'd best start north. I'd like to see nightfall find us across those hills and well on the way to Endeavour. Might even make it to town by dark, if we push them hard enough.'

'There's be no "pushing of them hard",' said the youngster coldly, 'Not after all they been through. This ain't the army and you're not leading men into battle. I say we find somewhere in those hills to hunker down for the night and then make the run for town early tomorrow morning.'

For a mere fraction of a second, Abe Merton felt fury coursing through him at hearing his plans challenged by this young puppy, but then he found himself admiring the boy for standing his ground. There was moreover something to be said for Ed's idea. If they embarked upon a forced march of fifteen miles or so, some of those girls were sure to faint or have the hysterics or some such.

Merton was also feeling a little guilty, because he had toyed with the idea of he and Hannah taking two of the mounts and then riding to town and fetching help, leaving the rest of the girls alone and unprotected. It would not be easy to think of a baser or less chivalrous action and he felt ashamed of even considering such a thing. He said to Ed, 'Have you thought of what will be needful if we are to ensure the safety of all the party?'

'I'd say gather up all the weapons and hand them out to the girls. Even if they can't all of them shoot straight, least they'd be able to make a noise and send some balls flying were we to be attacked.'

'It's well thought of. We'll make a soldier of you yet.'

There was no denying that the mood among the girls had vastly improved, now that they knew that they were free of the fear of being transported across the border into slavery. There was still hunger and exhaustion, of course, but their prospects for being returned safely to their families somehow made such hardships easier to endure. One of the girls had something on her mind, though, and sought out Abe Merton in order to beg the favour of a private word. It was Susan, who had clawed out the eyes of one of the Comancheros. When she and Merton were a little apart from the others and out of earshot, she said bluntly, 'Do you think as I was wrong to do what I done? Blindin' of that rascal, I mean.'

Merton did not answer for a space and the girl formed the mistaken impression that he was weighing her in judgement. She said, 'I don't see as there was anything more to be done, seeing that I had no weapon.'

To her surprise, the old man said, 'I done a sight worse than that in my time. You was in a tight corner and you did what you felt you had to. But having done so, you must feel mercy on that wretch. He's stone blind now and certain-sure to hang. I don't blame you none for injuring him so.'

'I was that scared and angry, but now it makes me sick to think on what I done.'

'You did what you had to do. There's no more to it than that. Try and set it out of your mind. You've no need to feel guilty in the least. Like I say, I've done worse. But what you do, you have to live with.'

To Abe Merton's boundless surprise, the girl, who seemed as hard as nails, came up and kissed him suddenly on the cheek, saying, 'You comfort me greatly. Thank you.'

Even with the girls taking turn and turn about on horseback, it was a slow journey. The party could only move at the pace of the slowest person on foot. The blinded man was able to walk, but the other two men, who had been wounded by Merton's mine, were in such a poor condition that Merton felt that he had to let them ride. The other injured bandit had died just before they set out, so no provision needed to be made for him.

It was coming on towards evening before they regained the hills and with at least another fifteen miles to go, it seemed pointless to hurry the pace. If they could cross the hills and be safe on the other side before stopping, then Merton felt that he would be satisfied. The more he thought on it, the more he believed in sending somebody to Endeavour so that some rescue could be attempted; the provision of wagons, perhaps. The idea of getting those girls to travel fifteen miles the following day on empty stomachs was not an attractive one.

One good thing when they reached the limestone hills was that everybody was able to slake his or her thirst to their heart's desire. The canteens had run dry and all the travellers, Merton included, were beginning to wonder how much longer they would be able to go in that heat without water. The first stream upon which they came was almost drained dry by the frantic rush of thirsty pilgrims. Once they had all drunk their fill, Merton took Ed Cherwell to one side and asked how well his sister was able to ride. 'Pretty well, I guess. We were both raised on a farm, you know.'

'How long would it take you to reach town from here? You and your sister both, if you were to ride as fast as you were able?'

'I don't rightly know. Two hours?'

'Would you consent to ride out now, this minute, with your sister? You could leave her there in safety, raise the alarm and arrange help. Then maybe you could race back here with some food.'

'I'd as soon not. She's shook up enough as it is. But what's to hinder one of those girls undertaking the same office? You could at least ask.'

Something about the idea of sending off a girl alone to fetch aid for them did not sit right with Merton, but it was true that they were in dire straits, and sometimes desperate situations call for desperate measures. Rather than make a general appeal, he went over to Susan after he had finished speaking with the boy, and said, 'May I have a few words with you?'

When the two of them were a little way off from the others, Merton said, 'You strike me as a young woman of sense and determination. Do you ride?'

'Good as a man, when they let me. Why?'

'I've an idea that you don't want to keep seeing the face of that man as you damaged, am I right?'

'Sure enough. Why?'

Abe Merton outlined what he had in mind, ending by saying, 'You don't have to take the commission unless you want. It's just an idea. You'd be removed from the painful necessity of seeing that fellow's eyes and also a good long ride might raise your spirits.'

'I'll do it.'

'Good girl, that's the way. You want to start right now? You could be in town in two hours, were you to ride fast.'

'I can ride fast.'

With the best will in the world, it was not likely that

128

any help would reach them before the next morning. It would take time for Susan to persuade the right people of what was needed and then there would be a deal of discussion and debate, but something would eventually be organised; of that Merton had no doubt.

After the girl had left, Merton and the boy guided the others through the pass that they had used themselves. By the time that the sun had set, they had gained the northern flank of the hills and there were perhaps a dozen or so miles to go before they got to the town of Endeavour. They should be able to achieve that distance on the morrow, but truth to tell, Merton was feeling mighty tired and ready to lay down the burden of responsibility for all those girls. He would be glad simply to slip off and see what he and Hannah were to do next. In all the fighting and mayhem, there had been no time to turn his mind to consideration of his future problems, but the time was surely not to be long delayed when this would become necessary.

When they had left Arkansas, Abe Merton had converted all his worldly goods into cash and then invested the entire sum in buying and fitting out a wagon to take him and his daughter west to California. Bar the hundred dollars in gold that he had brought with him to pay for food on the journey, that was it. The attack by the Comancheros had deprived him and his daughter of everything of

129

which they were possessed. Merton supposed that it was just about possible that the wagon still stood abandoned where the ambush had occurred, but even so, he would then need to acquire a couple of oxen and that would leave them with precious little in the way of money to buy provisions for the journey. Besides which, all their goods and chattels had been scattered on the highway and it would be little short of a miracle if others had not now looted the remainder of their belongings by now. What was to become of them, he really had not the least idea.

Abe Merton was not a man given overly much to introspection and brooding and so, knowing that for the present he and the boy were wholly responsible for the welfare and safety of sixteen girls and young women, he set to and performed what he conceived as his duty. He recollected the part of scripture that advises us to give no thought to the morrow and began establishing a camp, which he devoutly hoped would be the last night that he and these young people were obliged to spend in the wilderness.

Looked at from a purely rational point of view, the best that the three men who Ed Cherwell, Abe Merton and the girls had managed to drive away could hope for was to escape with their lives, and realize that their aims of making money from slavery had been well and truly dashed. Had they the sense that the Good Lord had given to a goat, they would have fled as fast as they were able and not looked back until they had crossed the Rio and were safely beyond reach of the law in Mexico. After the three of them were clear of the shooting and fighting that had taken place that day, though, this was not at all how the matter presented itself to them. No sooner had they galloped out of musket range and the danger of pursuit, than the three bandits had reined in and took counsel with each other.

What really stuck in them like a cocklebur was that an old man, a green boy and a bunch of girls had bested them. Had they clashed with a posse or army patrol and been obliged to flee, then that would have been one thing: a honourable defeat, as they might have seen it. This, though, was something else again. 'Why we didn't just shoot that old fellow out o' hand is more'n I can say,' said one. 'He's taken our women, killed our friends and left us like beggars. I ain't leaving it so, whatever you two want to do.'

'Them girls was like hellcats. If not for the part as they played, we might yet have come out on top.'

The third of them was of a more practical bent and after mulling things over, he said slowly, 'Happen things ain't as bad as we fear.'

'You taken leave o' your senses? We lost everything.'

'For now. There was a dozen of us going for to share what we made from them girls. How many were there?'

'Seventeen.'

'Well then, if we took back six of 'em and followed our plan, we'd be better off than we were before.'

None of them were subtle thinkers, nor for that matter able mathematicians, and it took the other two a little while to cipher out the figures. But if each girl was worth five hundred dollars or so, then before the disaster which had struck them, each of them had stood to gain somewhere in the region of six hundred and fifty dollars from the division of their spoils. If they now managed to acquire six girls and get them somehow over the river, then that would indeed give them a thousand dollars apiece. The man who had made this calculation pressed home his point of view. 'There's only that old fellow and the boy with him. What if we came on them by night and killed them and the chief part of the girls? Just took six of 'em and then made a run for the border? We'd be revenged for the death of our friends into the bargain.'

Set out in this way, the plan had many advantages and no visible disadvantages. They had been taken by surprise last time, both by the unexpected vigour of the man whose wagon they had ambushed and also by the violence of the girls. They would not make this mistake now. The choice was to walk away like dogs with their tails between their legs and not a cent to their name, or to fight back and find themselves in a better case than before: a thousand dollars each, rather than the six or seven hundred which they had been banking on. There was unanimous agreement on what needed to be done.

'Do you think that girl will come back here tonight with food?' asked Ed Cherwell of Merton. 'She might make it back ahead of a rescue party.'

'Struck me as she had more sense. I hope she stays in town and tries to recover.'

'Could you do what she did? Take out a man's eyes like that?'

'She did what she had to do. I'll set first watch tonight, but you'll have to relieve me about midnight. I don't get some sleep soon, I'm done for. I ain't as young as once I was and that's a fact.'

Although it had sounded a sensible scheme to arm the girls with the fallen enemies' weapons, when it came to the point, Merton felt distinctly uneasy about seeing firearms in the hands of fourteen- and fifteen-year-old girls. He saw one of them twirling a pistol round her finger by the trigger-guard, trying to make herself look like a fancy gunslinger and he called over irritably, 'What the deuce are you about there? That's not a toy!'

The girl blushed deeply and Merton repented of his sharp words. He went over to the child and said, 'Listen, you and the others have been right brave. But I'd be sorry if this ended with us shooting each other by accident after coming through so much. Set that pistol down now, like a good girl. If we are

133

attacked, then and only then do you need to take it up. Guns make good tools, but poor toys. You take my meaning?'

'Yes, sir.'

'Good girl.'

After going back to Ed, he said quietly, 'It'll be a mercy if none of us are shot by our own side at this rate.'

'I'll surely be glad to get back home again,' said the boy. 'Maybe some are suited to a life like this, but I'm not one of 'em. I'd rather be out ploughing than fighting like this. I always thought it would be exciting, you know. But it's not. It's just dirty.'

'Well,' replied Merton sensibly, 'At least you've found that out without having to sign up for years in the army, the way I did. Count yourself lucky. You've had a taste of adventure, found it don't suit you none and now you can get back home again. I'd say that was a good thing.'

'I guess. What will you and your daughter do now?'

'Scripture has it that "Morning brings counsel". I reckon I'd best see this night through and see if anything comes to me.'

'I'm sure my ma would be glad to see you and give you hospitality for a spell. If not for you, the Lord alone knows how this might have fallen out.'

'Let's see what the night brings and the morning after that. We ain't out of the woods yet, you know.'

At Merton's urging, all the others slept as soon as

it was full dark. They had eaten the last of their rations and there was no food left for the next day, but this had seemed a better idea to Merton than for them to try and sleep with empty bellies.

After everybody appeared to be sleeping, Merton prowled the camp like a restless ghost. He could not settle and although his ribs were paining him considerably, he feared to sit and relax, lest he should fall asleep himself. Besides which, notwithstanding all the evidence to the contrary, he could not quite rid himself of the sense that danger was still at hand. There seemed to be no reason for this feeling, but relying upon such feelings had saved his life more than once in the past, and so Merton did not disregard it now. He scanned the hills to the south uneasily, wondering what, if anything, might be amiss.

CHAPTER 8

Had Abe Merton but known it, his cat's sense for danger was serving him well that night. The army's activities in the north of Texas were yielding results, and the roving bands of Comancheros and their Kiowa allies were finding life a little uncomfortable, prompting a general drift south. Although the cavalry officer to whom he had spoken in Endeavour had not yet heard of it, a sharp engagement had lately been fought with a large force of Kiowa at the Palo Dura canyon. This resulted in the displacement of many warriors, who had been heading south since then, accompanied by not a few Comancheros. The plain around Endeavour was thus becoming a very hazardous place for any innocent people to traverse, as Abe Merton had found out to his cost a few days earlier.

Among those trying to evade the attention of the army was a group of Kiowa numbering about a hundred strong. These were not families driven from their homes, but lusty young braves who were, like the Comancheros, on the hunt and seeking easy prey. This band had reached the same hills near which Merton and his rescued girls were now camped and were, as Merton and his charges settled down for the night, sitting around fires some three or four miles to the east of them. The Indians had moved into the hills a little way, so that the twinkling of their campfires would not betray their position to any unfriendly watchers. Perhaps even at the distance that separated them, however, the faint tang of the burning wood had reached Merton's nostrils and, without realizing it consciously, had thus alerted him to the fact that there were others in the vicinity. As midnight approached, Abe Merton's sense of unease deepened and he had no intention of slumbering until he was assured that all was well.

Despite Merton's misgivings and slight anxiety he was bone-weary, and so when he judged by the Pole Star that it was about midnight, he awakened Ed Cherwell. After the youth was roused, Merton said, 'I've a feeling that all isn't well. Nothing I can explain, but you be sure not to fall asleep now, you hear what I tell you? First hint o' trouble and you wake me, all right?'

'Sure.'

In such casual ways are the fate of men and women sometimes decided, and a man's death brought about unwittingly. For the real danger in which the two men and the girls they were caring for lay not in the Kiowa camp a few miles to the east, but with three desperate and unscrupulous men who were so close to Merton and the boy that they overheard the very words of their conversation.

It had not been difficult for the three surviving members of the Comanchero gang who had been snatching girls to figure out the obvious: that the girls and their protectors would have to stop for a night before making on towards Endeavour. It was simply a matter of following carefully and quietly until they came upon them. Having caught sight of their quarry from the crest of a hill, it had simply needed patience to wait and see where they would stop for the night. The lower slopes of the hills were certainly a defensible location and the rings of boulders surrounding the sleepers would have been perfect had the girls been under attack in the broad light of day. As it was though, in pitch dark, those same boulders proved to be a blessing for those assaulting the camp, for they were enabled to creep up on all fours and secrete themselves within earshot of the people they meant to murder, and so be privy to their plans.

Even after he had supposedly handed over the watch to the youngster, Merton didn't feel that he could sleep with a clear conscience. He lay quietly for a while, staring up at the stars and trying not to worry about what would become of he and his daughter when this present escapade was over. Perhaps he would be able to find work in Endeavour and they could stay in that town for a spell, while he repaired the damage wrought to his affairs by those Comanchero scoundrels. It was the best that he could think of just then. He'd no resources in Arkansas, nor any intention to return there. It was while he was musing in this fashion, too tense and preoccupied with his troubles to sleep, that Merton became aware of a curious noise. At first, he thought that it might be some animal snuffling around the place in search of food. There was something a little too purposeful to the sound for that, though.

Raising his head slightly, Merton observed that Ed Cherwell was sitting erect upon a rock, his head moving back and forth, clearly alert to danger. Very slowly, Merton sat up as well and reached for the pistol that he invariably kept near his head when sleeping in the open. The furtive scratching and shuffling sounds had not abated and, unless he was very much mistaken, were now to be heard in more than one place on the periphery of the spot where they were camped. Either two or more large dogs or wolves were now creeping around them, or enemies were at hand. Merton cocked his pistol very slowly, not wishing to betray by any sharp sounds that he was about to go into battle.

Once again, Merton found that he had underesti-mated the boy he'd teamed up with, for Ed was now moving too. Among the arms belonging to the dead bandits had been a scattergun, a percussion-lock fowling piece, and it was this that the young man had seized upon as a weapon with which he was very familiar. Ed got to his feet, with the shotgun held at high port and ready to bring up to his shoulder as soon as he had identified a target. Ed saw Merton getting to his feet, by which he guessed correctly that the older man was also alarmed. The darkness made it impossible for either man to see the expression on the other's face, and the two of them were working by instinct. It was at that point, when Abe Merton stood up, that things began to get lively.

Just as Merton rose to his feet, a shadowy form emerged from one of the nearby rocks and, being sure that this was not one of the sleeping girls, Abe Merton hurled himself to one side. This exertion caused him exquisite pain in his cracked ribs. His action was worth this minor inconvenience, though, because even as he was moving to the ground, a shot rang out. As soon as he struck the rocky earth, Merton cocked his piece and turned to fire at the figure, which had now vanished. The awful fear now was that any blind shooting would result in the death of some of the girls, who were stirring and, in one or two cases, sitting upright in alarm. 'Stay down!' roared Merton. 'All you girls stay where are.'

Shouting out like that had caused Merton to reveal his position, for the next thing he knew somebody fired at him again, the ball passing closer than was comfortable past his head. Then came the dull boom of a scattergun, which Merton assumed was young Ed shooting at somebody. He seemed to be having more success than Merton was, because before the echo of the shot had died away, a cry of pain could be heard. Mind, with a shotgun, this could be no more than somebody being stung by a few stray bits of buckshot; it didn't mean that anybody was badly hurt.

It was the very devil trying to find and dispose of enemies like this in pitch dark. There was no use standing around like a tailor's dummy, thought Merton, and so he ran, jinking from side to side, towards the boulders that surrounded them. He'd a notion that whoever the attackers were, they had been creeping up on the camp and were now crouching on the other side of the rocks. It was in this way that he suddenly found himself almost face to face with a man who had chosen that moment to poke his head up and peer over a boulder the size of a barrel to see what the play was. This was no time for playing things slowly and carefully, and so Abe Merton simply shot the fellow down, the ball striking the man as far as he could gauge, smack between his eyes. That was one less, at any rate.

Then there began a very confused and violent few seconds, because a flurry of movement to his left indicated to Merton that one of those assaulting them had leapt into their midst and was trying to drag off one of the girls. She screamed out, 'Ed, Ed, help me!' He understood that this was most likely Ed Cherwell's sister, Martha. Before he could shout for the boy to stay put, young Ed came bounding towards the cry for help. At that precise moment, a shot rang out and the running figure of the young man faltered and then tumbled forward. Merton strode forward, sensing that the man who had hold of Martha had his back to Merton. This proved to be so, because as he reached the struggling pair, the shadowy figures resolved themselves into a tall man, grasping a slender figure that was struggling to escape. Rather than fire and risk hitting the girl, Merton grabbed the fellow by the arm and jerked him loose. Then he shot him down like the dog he was.

The whole place had become a hubbub of con-fused shouting and crying. Mingled with the frightened wailing of the girls could be heard the hoarse cries of the wounded Comanchero prisoners, shouting such things as, 'Over here, fellows!' and 'Come and help me get free!' Merton had taken the precaution of tying the hands of both the men he had captured, even the one who had been blinded. A little way off, the horses were also whinnying and neighing in terror. Merton crouched down and simply waited, turning his head all the time for any sign of movement. When it came, the silhouette of the man clambering over the rocks seemed as good a target as he was likely to find that night, and so he cocked his pistol and fired twice at the man. Judging by the way that the figure jerked each time he fired, like a marionette having its strings tugged, Merton took it that his shooting was as good as usual, even in this Stygian gloom.

After waiting a minute and finding that there was no further sign of any enemies, Merton got to his feet and went over to where he had seen Ed Cherwell fall. His sister was there as well, talking to her brother in a low, tearful voice. He squatted beside the boy and said, 'Well, how goes it, young Ed?'

'I'm hurt real bad, sir. My arms and legs feel cold and it pains me to breathe.'

'Tush! That's just the shock o' being shot. It took me the same way, first time I stopped a ball. Let's strike a light and see what's what. Stay where you are.'

Merton picked his way over the prone figures and went past the ring of rocks to where the horse had been left hobbled. After finding the one that he had been riding, he fumbled around in the saddle-bag until he found a box of matches. Then he returned to see what the damage was to the young boy. It was much worse than he had supposed, despite his cheery assurances to the injured youth.

Striking one of the Lucifers showed at once that a bullet had struck the boy low in his stomach and then exited near his spine. If Merton was any judge of such matters, the ball had caused some harm to the backbone as it left the youngster's body, in addition to whatever havoc it had wrought as it ploughed through his vitals. The grave expression on his face must have betrayed him, for Ed said, 'It's like I said, ain't it? I'm hurt bad.'

He didn't have the heart to lie to the boy, nor would it have been a kindness at this point. Merton said slowly, 'I'm no sawbones, but I should just about say you were right, son.'

There was a long pause, broken only by Martha Cherwell's weeping and lamentations at hearing this blunt opinion. Abe Merton continued, 'Don't you fret about your sister. I'll take good care of her and see as she gets home safe to your ma.' He felt that he should add something and said, 'We did well together, me and you. I can tell you now, you was the best comrade a man might ask for on such an expedition. It's been a pleasure riding with you.'

Merton lit another match. Ed's face was drawn and white, but he was smiling in appreciation of what he had said. Then, in the manliest way imaginable, without any fuss or wailing, he simply departed this life as Merton and the boy's sister watched. He drew one, long, last shuddering breath and then let it out slowly and gently. He did not breathe again.

'Well,' said Merton quietly, 'He's been promoted to glory. He was a good man.'

He thought it fitting to sit in silence for a space

besides the boy's corpse, but there was so obviously a deal that needed his attention that after five or ten or ten seconds, Merton patted Martha's hand in what he hoped was a comforting fashion, and then got to his feet. He went first to where the three bound prisoners lay and, leaning over them, said vindictively, 'Your partners killed a boy. Best young man I met in a good long while. I'll make certain-sure all of you hang, you have my oath on it.'

In addition to his genuine grief at the death of Ed Cherwell, Merton had another feeling: that of being completely alone and having nobody to aid him in what was next to be done. Without noticing, he had come to rely a little upon the youngster who lay dead and he now knew that the lives of the seventeen girls depended entirely upon he himself. It was a lonely enough sensation. True, Hannah was there, but Abednego Merton had grown up at a time when men relied only upon other men, not upon their womenfolk, however capable and able to wield a firearm those women might be. As he stared into the inky blackness he felt utterly alone. He tried to pray, but even that comfort was denied him. For once, he did not feel the presence of the Lord near at hand.

The Pole Star had scarce moved since he'd roused young Ed for his watch, by which Merton took it that the hour couldn't be much past one in the morning. Although he had been desperately tired before he laid down, he found now that he was as wide awake as could be and there seemed little point in laying his self down to toss and turn restlessly. Instead, he sat on a rock and turned over what the morning might bring. Surely, if that young woman had reached Endeavour yesterday afternoon, then some attempt to reach him and his charges would be launched early in the morning that was fast approaching? Leastways, he hoped that this was so.

Hannah, who was evidently also not sleepy, came over to her father and said, 'I'm sorry about that young fellow, Pa. I could see you liked him.'

'He was a game one, I'll say that. Yes, I'm sorry that he's dead. Let's hope he was right with the Lord and supping now in the Promised Land.'

His daughter obviously had something to say, but was not sure how to broach the subject. Merton had no patience for shilly-shallying and said, 'Come, child, out with it. What's troubling you?'

'Are we still going to California? We're not bound for Arkansas, are we?'

'Truth to tell, I don't yet know what will befall us, but we ain't heading back to Arkansas, that I can tell you. Maybe, though, it'll take a little longer to reach the west coast than we first hoped for. That answer your question?'

'I reckon.'

'Go and get some sleep, there's a good girl. I don't yet know what awaits us when the sun rises.'

The night passed slowly, the hours crawling by like

146

snails. One thing that Merton especially noticed was that the sense of unease he had felt the previous evening had not abated in the slightest degree; he still had the apprehension that danger was near at hand. It might have been thought that with the successful defence that had driven off the remnants of the Comanchero band, Abe Merton would have felt better, but whatever it was which had troubled him earlier was still there. He knew without a shadow of doubt that some threat still hung over the girls whom he was tending.

At first light, the old man toured the camp, finding that in addition to Ed Cherwell, there were four other corpses to be considered. Three were of strangers, presumably those who had attacked in the dead of night. One of the wounded men had also died in the night, leaving only two prisoners for him to concern himself with.

As soon as the sun rose, Merton bellowed 'Good morning!' so loudly that it would have awoken the dead. The girls stirred and then began sitting up and looking about them. Merton said in a loud voice, 'There's no breakfast to be had, so when you girls have tended to your needs, we'll be on our way. Quickly now.'

There was some grumbling at the brisk and autocratic way in which Merton made this announcement, but he had a powerfully strong feeling that they should not be lingering near those hills for much longer. If rescuers from Endeavour were on their way, then they might meet each on the way. There was little chance of missing anybody on the broad, flat plain that stretched away to the horizon.

Ed Cherwell's body was slung over the saddle of one horse; Merton had no intention of leaving the boy to be devoured by wild animals. The least he could do was return his body to the grieving mother who probably thought that she had lost two children by now. At least he would have the pleasure of returning one of her children to her safe and sound. The blind man was set to walk again, being guided by a length of rope attached to the saddle of one of the mounts. Abe Merton made sure to keep a sharp eye on this fellow, for he would not have put it past him to make a bolt for it, even now. If Merton had any say in it, this man would be delivered up to justice.

The weary girls, some on horseback and the rest trudging along on foot, set off from the flank of the hill a little after the sun had broken free of the distant horizon. They had not gone more than a half-mile or so when Merton observed that a number of riders were bearing down on them from the east. The risen sun was in his eyes and so he could not identify them, seeing only the pale, grey haze of the dust that they were kicking up to hang in the still air. From the size of the cloud, he guessed that the riders must number in scores, maybe as many as a hundred.

Just as he was making this calculation, the faint sound of warbling cries of triumph reached him. Unless he was greatly mistaken, these were Indians and their shouts indicated that they had spotted Merton and his girls.

It was bitter to have made it so far and then to fall, as it were, at the final hurdle. Still, there it was. This at least explained the feelings that had troubled him the night before. Somehow, these men must have given some sign of their close proximity and he had heard, seen or smelled something that warned him of their presence unconsciously. Well, that was nothing to the purpose. He supposed that all that remained was to see that they sold their lives as dearly as could be.

Merton said, 'All you girls as have weapons, get them out and ready yourselves to fire. We're apt to have company shortly.'

As he was musing on whether there was anything else to be done, there came through the chill, morning air the last sound that anybody could have expected: the faint, brassy note of a bugle. Hardly daring to hope, Abe Merton turned his head around and saw that to the northwest, where the sky was still dark, another body of horsemen was heading in their direction. Because the sky was still a deep blue over there, the dust kicked up by these riders had not attracted attention in the way that that hanging in the eastern sky had done.

It was hard to say which of the groups of riders would reach them first, but the Indians looked now to be changing direction. Instead of heading straight for Merton and his girls, they were veering off to the left, clearly wishing to engage with the cavalry. The two forces met about half a mile from Merton and so he and the others were treated to a grandstand view of what was to prove one of the biggest clashes in the Texas Indian wars, until the battle of Palo Dura five years later. It was as good as a play to watch the mounted riders crash into each other, the cavalry troopers swinging their sabres and the Kiowa warriors with their lances and tomahawks. The eventual outcome wasn't really in any doubt, for the Indian braves were outnumbered by at least two to one. Merton guessed that these must be the soldiers who he had seen camped by Endeavour. He had thought at the time that there must have been at least two hundred men there and every one of them must be here now.

It was a magnificent sight and one which Merton, as an old soldier, found particularly stirring, but the fighting lasted no more than five or ten minutes, before the surviving Indians cut and ran, leaving behind on the field of battle at least half their number. The cavalry made no attempt to pursue them but, at a signal from the bugler, reformed and trotted in parade-ground order towards Merton and the girls. When they were close enough to recognize individual men, Merton saw that the unit was commanded by the major who he had talked to a few days earlier. He hailed the officer and said, 'So you decided to come and help us after all, hey?'

'We didn't come all the way out here for you folks,' replied the major, when he was a little closer. 'We had a crow to pluck with those Kiowa and received word that they were on the rampage in these parts. Been driven out of Palo Dura. But I hear that some people from town are heading here to relieve you. I can spare a few men to guard you until they arrive, if that would be agreeable?'

'I can't think of anything better, Major. We'd be mighty obliged to you.'

It was several hours before some of the townsfolk fetched up with carts and spare mounts. The girls were all able to travel to Endeavour in some comfort, but Merton and Hannah chose to ride. Martha accompanied them. The horses that they had been using were linked together with rope, and Merton led them behind. He even consented to allow his two prisoners to ride.

When they arrived back in town, there were no end of questions to be answered and Abe Merton found himself the unwilling centre of attention. Susan had already given a lurid account of the role that he had played in their rescue and the other girls, once they arrived in town, could hardly praise him enough. All this was most unwelcome for Merton, who preferred to live a quiet and unassuming life.

More interesting to him than becoming the object of the town's gratitude and admiration was the discovery of a pair of US Marshals in charge of a cage on wheels; some kind of gaol delivery. From what he could make out, the job of these men was collecting captured criminals and transporting them to the big town of Santa Maria a few miles to the east.

There were four men in the travelling gaol, all of whom were shackled and looked as unprepossessing a bunch of customers as you could hope to meet. Merton led his string of horses, two of which were burdened with his prisoners, up to where the marshals were standing and chatting with a couple of soldiers. He went up to the little group and said, 'I've two men here, all that remains of them as have been taking girls to sell into slavery.'

'The devil you have!' exclaimed one of the marshals in amazement. 'You mean these two?'

'I do.'

'Well now, me and this'un,' said the marshal, indicating one of Merton's prisoners, 'We know each other. Don't we, Mister Gonzalez? You might say that we're old friends.' The man on horseback, one of those injured in the explosion that Merton had set off, said nothing, merely scowling.

The marshal turned to Merton and said, 'Fact is, we've been hoping to speak to this fellow for the longest time. Little matter of murder, robbery and suchlike.'

'You want him on a capital charge?'

'Oh yes, it's a hanging matter all right, don't you fret none about that. There's a reward too.'

Abednego Merton might have been a God-fearing man who was only doing his duty by handing this villain over to the law, but he was a father too, anxious about the welfare of his daughter, given the loss of his wagon. He said, 'You reckon I'm entitled?'

'Nobody more, since you've taken him and delivered him up.'

'I ain't a bounty hunter, you know.'

'Never said you were. There's five hundred dollars payable for Mister Gonzalez, and it's yours if you want it.'

During the course of this conversation, the other marshal had been staring hard at the blinded Comanchero. He took from his pocket a large sheet of paper, which was folded up small, and opened it out. He proceeded to stare at this, glancing up occasionally at the man seated on the horse. Then he went over to the marshal to whom Abe Merton was talking and showed him the sheet of paper in such a way that Merton could not see what it was. 'You reckon that's him?' asked one of the lawmen to the other.

'One way to check for sure,' replied the other, gesturing to the paper, which Merton guessed was a wanted poster or something similar. One of the marshals went over to where the man with the ruined eyes sat astride the horse and touched him on the arm. 'Roll up your right sleeve,' said the marshal, 'Right up to the shoulder.'

'Why?' said the prisoner. 'Why should I?'

' 'Cause if you don't, we'll knock you off your mount and do it for you.'

Slowly and with every sign of reluctance, the man unbuttoned his cuff and rolled his sleeve up as far as the elbow. 'There, that good enough for you?'

'A bit further, if you please.'

Once the fellow's sleeve was clear of the elbow, a blue line could be seen on his bicep. One marshal reached out and pulled the fabric further, to reveal a curious tattooed design, something like a mono-gram. Both lawmen looked satisfied and nodded meaningfully. One turned to Merton and said, 'Well, sir, I reckon your luck's in today, no matter what you've had to go through. This fellow is Raymonde Delgado, and he's wanted in a dozen places from what this here bill tells. The price on him is a thousand dollars.'

'You mean that's mine as well?' asked Abe Merton in amazement.

'You delivered him to us, didn't you? Only point is, we ain't got such an amount of cash money about us. Where you headed?'

'California. We was aiming to stop over in El Paso.'

'Well, there's a line from Santa Maria over to El Paso. When we get there, we can wire authority for the office in El Paso to pay out.' The man took out a pad and after asking Merton his name and various other things, wrote out a chit laboriously and signed it. He said, 'Present this to the marshal's office in El Paso and they'll pay out your cash. Give us a week, though, to arrange it all at Santa Maria.'

CHAPTER 9

So rapid had been the change in fortune that Abednego Merton felt a little giddy. A moment earlier, he had been thinking that he and his daughter would be trapped in Endeavour until he had earned enough money to buy a new wagon. Now, it seemed that all they need do was ride to El Paso and there would be enough money waiting there for him to purchase another wagon and equip it. If that wasn't the hand of the Lord at work, rewarding his servant, then he didn't know what it was. Whether or no, it was a great weight off his mind to know that he and Hannah would be able to forge on to El Paso with no delay.

There remained one final and melancholy duty to perform. Neither of the two marshals was interested in the horses belonging to the dead Comancheros and suggested to Merton that he had as good a right to them as anybody, and that if he wanted to sell

156

them and pocket the money then they were happy with such an arrangement. He disposed of all except four of the beasts: one each for him and Hannah, one for young Martha and another to bear the corpse of her brave, dead brother.

As they followed Martha's direction to her home, the farm where she had lately been living peacefully with her brother, Merton said to her, 'Listen, child, your mother'll be wild with joy to see you back home safe and sound. When we're in sight of your home, you get down and run ahead, see? Least she'll have the joy of seeing you back before we have to tell her about that brother of yours.'

'I haven't thanked you properly, sir. . . .' began the girl.

Abe Merton cut in brusquely, saying, 'You've no need to thank me. I let your brother die and that's a heavy burden on me. It was he who wouldn't give up. You owe your life to him, not me.'

It was all just as Merton had thought. Martha's mother was working in a vegetable plot at back of their little house. When she caught sight of her daughter, the woman screamed with joy and ran helter-skelter to her child, enfolding her in her arms. For a few moments, she was utterly overjoyed to have the child back safely. Then she looked up, plainly wondering where her son was. Although he had taken care to keep the horse bearing its grisly burden shielded a little from sight, there was no deceiving a mother's instincts. She guessed from the sober look on Abe Merton's face what the truth was, and for a moment looked as though she was about to collapse in a heap. Merton said to his daughter, 'Go tend to her, Hannah. This needs a woman's hand.'

A curious circumstance that later struck Merton was that this was the first time he had ever referred to his daughter, or even thought of her, as a woman. Watching how tenderly Hannah helped Martha's mother into her house, though, it was clear that this was no child but somebody on the very cusp of womanhood, which was a sobering thought indeed. Hannah had always hitherto been his little girl. Time, he reckoned, to acknowledge that she was changing and that before long they would be two grown people, rather than just father and child, as it had been since time out of mind. That would take some thinking on and no mistake!

There was little that they could do to help the widow Cherwell, other than to spend a little time consoling and commiserating with her. Before they left, the grieving mother said to Merton, 'Was he . . . my Ed, you know . . . was he brave?'

'I've had a heap o' partners, ma'am, but I can tell you now that he was one of the best men I ever rode with. I trusted him with my life and I'm only sorry I couldn't save him. He gave his life for his sister.'

Ed's mother clutched Merton's hand wordlessly and could not bring herself to speak when they parted. He only wished that he could have done more than deliver her son's lifeless corpse to her. It felt kind of strange, depositing the body in the barn like that, but maybe she had good neighbours who might help her with the digging of a grave and so on.

Now, though, it was time for him and his daughter to head back to town. Merton reckoned that they deserved a proper bed for the night, if they could find somebody to rent them a room or two. Then, in the morning, they would head west again. He only hoped that the rest of the journey would prove more peaceable.